THE NEW FANTASY NOVEL FROM SAMUEL R. DELANY!

"Bringing out new early Delany is the publishing equivalent of extracting dinosaur DNA from flies embedded in amber. Would that there were more!"

—William Gibson

"In his lovely and, yes, soaring descriptions of the Winged Ones of Hi-Vator, Delany seems to be giving free reign to a joy and sheer love of the marvelous . . . Plus his winged creatures have a naughty sex game they play while airborne, and who can't relate to *that*?"

—Elizabeth Hand

"Vintage Delany in his finest fantasy mode: a violent tale that is also a mature and tender meditation on violence."

—Ursula K. Le Guin

"Delany's prose is subtle and deep enough that attempting to describe the book is like trying to portray a rainbow in black and white. It's well worth reading—and re-reading."

—L.E. Modesitt, Jr.

"*They Fly At Çiron* has the unmistakable stamp of Samuel R. Delany. Like everything he writes, it's subtle, surprising, involving, and above all, beautifully written."

—Connie Willis

D0681455

BOOKS BY SAMUEL R. DELANY

FICTION:

The Jewels of Aptor
The Fall of the Towers:
    Out of the Dead City
    The Towers of Toron
    City of a Thousand Suns
The Ballad of Beta-2
Babel-17
Empire Star
A Fabulous, Formless Darkness (The Einstein
   Intersection)
Nova
Driftglass (stories)
Equinox (The Tides of Lust)
Dhalgren
Triton
Distant Stars (stories)
Stars in My Pocket like Grains of Sand
Return to Nevèrÿon:
    Tales of Nevèrÿon
    Neveryóna
    Flight from Nevèrÿon
    Return to Nevèrÿon (The Bridge of Lost
       Desire)
They Fly at Çiron
Driftglass / Starshards (collected stories)
The Mad Man
Atlantis: Model 1924

NONFICTION:

The Jewel-Hinged Jaw
The American Shore
Heavenly Breakfast
Starboard Wine
The Motion of Light in Water
Wagner / Artaud
The Straits of Messina
Silent Interviews

THEY FLY AT ÇIRON

SAMUEL R. DELANY

TOR
fantasy ®

A TOM DOHERTY ASSOCIATES BOOK
NEW YORK

THEY FLY AT ÇIRON

Copyright © 1993 by Samuel R. Delany

All rights reserved, including the right to reproduce this book, or portions thereof, in any form.

"They Fly at Çiron" first appeared, in a different, much shorter version, as "They Fly at Çiron," by Samuel R. Delany and James Sallis, in *The Magazine of Fantasy & Science Fiction,* June 1971, Vol. 40, No. 6, pp. 32–60. Copyright © 1971 by Mercury Press, Inc.

"Ruins" has appeared twice previously, in versions slightly different from one another and from the one in the present volume: as "In the Ruins," by Samuel R. Delany, in *Algol,* No. 13, January 1968, Copyright © 1968 by Andrew Porter; and as "Ruins," in *Distant Stars* by Samuel R. Delany (Bantam Books, New York: 1981), pp. 279–291, Copyright © 1981 by Samuel R. Delany.

A trade and a limited edition of *They Fly at Çiron* were first published by Incunabula, Seattle, 1993.

Cover art by Thomas Canty

A Tor Book
Published by Tom Doherty Associations, Inc.
175 Fifth Avenue
New York, N.Y. 10010

Tor Books on the World-Wide Web:
http://www.tor.com

Tor® is a registered trademark of Tom Doherty Associates, Inc.

ISBN: 0-812-54317-3
Library of Congress Card Catalog Number: 94-38152

First Tor edition: January 1995
First Tor mass market edition: February 1996

Printed in the United States of America

0 9 8 7 6 5 4 3 2 1

For
  Dennis Rickett
and with thanks to
  Sam DeBenedetto,
  Leonard Gibbs,
  & Don Eric Levine.

NOTE

I first wrote "They Fly at Çiron" as a forty-five-page story in my second-floor flat at the dead end of East 5th Street. From my spiral notebooks I typed the first version on a mechanical typewriter in late spring '62. My editor did not buy it, however; nor was I really satisfied with the tale. Sometime toward 1969 I gave the MS to my friend James Sallis. Jim reworked the opening. That version appeared as a collaboration under our paired bylines in the June '71 issue of *The Magazine of Fantasy & Science Fiction*. Twenty years later, though, it struck me that the story could still use a pass through the word processor. When I was done, I had a hundred-fifty-page manuscript. For all I've added, I've kept none of Jim's inventive amendments. Nevertheless they formed an invaluable critique, defining lacks I've now addressed otherwise. As none of Jim's language remains, I can no longer reprint *They Fly at Çiron* as a proper collaboration. But neither can I publish it—far truer for this than for the '71 version—without ackowledging that critique responsible for anything now in it worth the reading. In 1992, equally detailed critiques of the new version came from Randy Byers and Ron Drummond. And, in my sunny Amherst study, I responded here and there to them the best I could—and the manuscript is fifty pages longer. In one sense, this is my second novel—only it has taken me thirty years to write.

—S.R.D.

CONTENTS

PROEM

Among the tribes and villages and hamlets and
   townships
that ornament the world with their variety,
   many have existed
in mutual support, exchange, and friendship.
   Many others
have stayed to themselves, regarding their
   neighbors
with unease, hostility, and suspicion. Some
   have gone
from one state to the other. Some have even
   gone back.
But when the memory of a village is no older
   than the four
or five generations it takes a grave-scroll
   record to rot,
there *is* no history—only myth and song. And
   the truth is,

while a minuscule number of these may echo
   down the ages,
only a handful endure more than a season; and
   the vast majority
from such handfuls linger (listen to the songs
   and myths
about you!) less than a lifetime.

CHAPTER
ONE

They are dogs."

"My prince—"

"They are less than dogs. Look: they inch on their stomachs, like maggots."

"Prince Nactor, they are men—men who fought bravely against us—"

"—and whom we vanquished, Lieutenant Kire." The prince slipped long fingers through the fence's diamond-crossed wires—and grasped. "That gives me the right to do anything I want to them." With his free hand, still in its leather gauntlet, he lifted his powergun from its sling. "Anything."

"My prince, yours is also the right to be merciful—!"

"Even this, Kire." Nactor put the barrel-end through the wire. "Now watch." The first time he fired, the two who could still scream started in again. Another—who could move—dragged himself over the dirt, took hold of the fence wire, and tried to pull himself up. His fingers caught. Silently, he opened his mouth, and closed it, and opened it. Nactor glanced back, grinning through his beard. "Smells like barbecue, doesn't it?" Turning again, he thrust the barrel between the wires into the prisoner's eye.

The gun and the fence both jumped at the report.

Charred neck and bloody hands slid to the ground.

He took out the noisiest two last, some forty seconds apart. During those seconds, while the smoke above the fence settled back down, Nactor began to smile. The one huddling into himself opened his eyes, then squeezed them tight—he was making a sound more between a wheeze and a whine than a scream. Nactor's beard changed its shape a little as, behind it, his face seemed to grow compassionate. He leaned toward the wire, as though at last he saw something human, something alive, something he could recognize.

Without stopping the sound, the prisoner began to blink.

Nactor lowered the gun.

The man finally let an expression besides terror twitch through the scabs and the mud; he took a breath . . .

Nactor thrust the gun through—and shot.

The fence jumped.

A hand, charred now, slid through the muck. Something no longer a face splatted down.

Nactor reslung his weapon and turned from

the corral, releasing the wire. "I find killing
these"—the fence vibrated—"easier than
those creatures from their cave-holdings that
we exterminated three attacks ago. These at
least were human. But those, with their shaggy
pelts and their thickened nails like beast
claws—I suppose they reminded me of my dogs
at home. There, your requests for clemency,
your sour looks and your sulkings, really got
on my nerves, Kire. This was worth doing just
to keep you quiet." He glanced where Kire's
hand jerked, now toward, now away from, the
sling at his own hip. "That is, if it doesn't actually cheer you up. Lieutenant?" (Three more
jerks, and Kire's arm, in its black sleeve,
straightened.) "Is it really necessary to remind
you that the purpose of this expedition is con-
quest—that Myetra must expand His bound-
aries, or He will perish? When the time comes
for our final encounter with Calvicon, you will
. . . I *trust* you will distinguish yourself in war,
in service to Myetra, bringing honor to your
superiors, who watch you, and to your men,
who trust you." The prince palmed the powergun's handle, moving gauntleted fingers on the
sling's silver embossing, worked into Kirke,
Myetra's totemic crow. (The silver came from
the Lehryard mines; the guns were smithed in
the Tradk Mountains. For both guns and silver, Myetra traded wheat taken by force from
the veldt villages of Zeneya. Even Kirke, Kire
reflected, had come from a distant county he
could no longer name, but which Myetra had
long ago laid waste to.) "What is our mission
now, Kire? Just so I know you haven't forgotten: To march our troops across this land in a

line as straight as . . . as what?"

" 'As straight as a blood drop down a new-plastered wall.' " The Lieutenant's voice was low, measured, but with some roughness in it that might have been a social accent, an emotional timbre, or a simple failure in the machinery of tongue, throat, and larynx. "Shoen, Horvarth, Nutting, and fourteen other hamlets lie devastated behind us. Çiron, Hi-Vator, Requior and seven more villages lie ahead to be crushed, before we reach Calvicon for our final encounter."

The prince raised his gloved hand and with his naked forefinger began to tick off one, two, three . . . : "Yes, it *is* seven. I thought it was eight there, for a moment. You might almost think I wanted to prolong the pleasures of this very pleasant journey we've been on almost a year and half now. But you're right. It's only seven. The best way to spill blood in war, Kire, is to spill it where all can see. You spill it slowly, Kire—slowly, so that the enemy has time to realize our power and our greatness, the greatness of Myetra. Some locales have a genius for work, for labor, for toiling and suffering. And some have a genius for ruling. Myetra . . . !" The prince flung up his gauntleted fist in salute. Lowering it, however, a smile moved behind his heavy beard that put all seriousness into question. "There really is no other way." With his ungloved knuckles, the prince pushed his rough beard hair to shape, now forward from his ears, now back at his chin. "Those who disagree, those who think there is another way, are Myetra's enemies. You've seen how merciful Myetra is to its enemies, eh,

Kire—?" Abruptly, Prince Nactor turned and walked toward his tent.

In his black undergarments, black jerkin with black leggings over them, black harness webbing hips and chest, black hood tight around his face (a scimitar of bronze hair had slipped from under the edge), and wearing an officer's night-colored·cape that did not rise anywhere as high as you might expect in the steady, eastern breeze, the tall lieutenant· turned.too—after a breath—and walked from the corral.

The troops sat at fires paled to near·invisibility by the silvery sun. Some men cleaned their weapons. Others talked of the coming march. One or two still ate. A stack of·armor flung a moment's glare in Kire's eyes, brighter than the flames.

In only his brown undershorts, cross-legged and hunched over a roasted rabbit haunch, the little soldier, Mrowky, glanced up to call: "Lieutenant Kire, come eat—"

His belly pushing down the waist of his undershorts, the hem of his singlet up, standing by the fire big Uk said: "Hey, Lieutenant—?"

On the ground, Mrowky lifted freckled shoulders. "Sir, we saved some hare—"

But Kire strode on to the horse enclosure, where two guards quickly uncrossed their spears—and flung up their fists. (Kire thought: How little these men know what goes on in their own camp.) He stepped between them and inside, reached to pull down a bridle, bent to heft up a saddle. He cut out his mare, threw the leather over her head, put the saddle over her back, and bent beneath her belly for the cinch. A black boot in the iron stirrup, and moments later he galloped out, calling: "I shall be back before we decamp for Çiron."

Passing loudly, wind slapped at his face—but could not fill his cape to even the gentlest curve. Hooves hit up dirt and small stones, crackled in furze. Low foliage snapped by. The land spun back beneath.

Dim and distant, the Çironian mountains lapped the horizon. Kire turned the horse into a leafy copse. A branch raked at him from the right. Twigs with small leaves brushed his left cheek as he pulled—in passing—away. The mare stepped about; behind them brush and branches rushed back into place. At a stream, Kire jabbed his heels into the mare's flanks, shook the reins—

—an instant later, with four near-simultaneous clops, hooves hit the rockier shore. Pebbles spattered back into the water. Kire rode forward, to mount a rise and halt there, bending to run a black glove on the flat neck. He was about to canter down among the trees, when a long and inhuman *Screeeeee* made the horse rear. Kire reined hard and tightened his black leggings against her flanks.

Raucous and cutting, the *Screee* came again. The mare danced sideways.

Dismounting, Kire dropped the reins to the ground. Snorting twice, the mare stilled.

Upper leg bending and lower leg out, Kire crabbed the slope, coming down in a sideways slide around a boulder.

Startlingly closer, the *Screeeeee* sliced low leaves.

Kire stepped around broken stone, stopped—and breathed in:

A man, a beast—

Yellow claws slashed at a brown shoulder. The shoulder jerked—the head ducked; black hair flung up and forward. Bodies locked. Braced on the ground, a bare foot gouged through pine needles.

Canines snapped toward a wrist that snatched away to lash around behind the puma's neck. This time, as the *Screeeee* whined between black gums and gray, gray teeth, something . . . cracked!

A broad paw clapped the man's side—but the sound failed. The claws had retracted.

Kire let his air out as puma and man, one dead, one exhausted, toppled onto their shadows.

Before Kire got in another breath, another shadow slid across them. On the ground, the man raised himself to one arm, and shook back long hair. Kire stepped forward—to see the shadow around them get smaller and darker. He reached for the man's shoulder. At the same time, he looked up.

The flying thing—sun behind it burned on one wing's edge: Kire could see only its size— dropped. Kire's gun-barrel cleared the sling. The report ripped the air . . . though the shot went wild.

Above, it averted, wings glinting like chipped quartz, then flapped up to soar away.

At Kire's feet, the naked man rocked on all fours by the beast.

"It's gone, now," Kire rasped. "Get up."

The man pushed himself back on his knees,

taking in great breaths through lips pulled up from large, yellow teeth. Then he stood.

He was taller than Kire by a hand. A good six years younger too, the lieutenant decided, looking at the wide, brown face, the hair sweated in black blades to a cheek and a forehead still wrinkled with gasps from the fight. The eyes were molten amber—wet and hot.

(The lieutenant's eyes were a cool, startling green.)

Pulling up his cape and throwing it over his arm, Kire reslung his gun. "Who are you?"

"Rahm." Still breathing hard, he reached up with wide fingers to brush dirt and puma hair from his heaving chest and rigid belly. "Rahm of Çiron." The lips settled to a smile. "I thank thee for frightening away the Winged One with thy . . ." He motioned toward Kire's black waist-cinch.

"This is my powergun." The tall youngster's dialect, Kire noted, was close to Myetra's. "Rahm . . ." The Lieutenant snorted; it sounded like a continuation of whatever roughened his voice. "Of Çiron, 'ey?"

The Çironian's smile opened up. "That is a . . . powergun? It's a frightening thing, the . . . powergun." He moved his head: from where it clawed and clutched his shoulder, black hair slid away. "And who art thou, that hast become Rahm's friend?"

"I am Kire." He did not give his origin, though with Kirke on left breast, cloak, and sling, he could not imagine the need.

"Thou art a stranger in these lands," Rahm said. "Whither dost thou travel?"

"Soon to the Çironian mountains. But for

now, I am merely a wanderer, looking at the land about me, to learn what I can of it."

"So am I—or so I have been. But now I am returning to Çiron." Suddenly the black-haired youth bent, grabbed the puma's yellow foreleg, and tugged. "Here." He thrust one dark foot against pale stomach-fur to shove the beast over the pine needles. With its closed eyes, the puma's head rolled aside, as if for the moment it wished to avoid the bright, brown gaze of its murderer. "Thou shouldst have the lion, for saving me from the Winged One. I had thought to carry it home—it's no more than three hours' walk. But thou hast a horse." He nodded up the slope. " 'Tis thine."

Kire felt a smile nudge among his features. "Thank you." A smile was not the expression he'd thought to use with this Çironian youth. So he stepped back, to lean against the boulder. "Rahm . . . ?" Kire glanced at the sky, then back. "How is it you travel the land naked and without a weapon?"

Rahm shrugged. "The weather is warm. My arms are strong." Here he frowned. "A weapon . . . ?"

"You don't know what a weapon is . . ."

Rahm shook his head.

"Suppose you had not been able to kill the puma with your bare hands . . . ?"

"Eventually she would have gotten frightened and fled—once I'd hurt her enough." The youth laughed. "Or she would have killed me. But that could not happen. I am stronger than any animal in this land—except, perhaps, the Winged Ones."

"And what are they?"

"They live in the mountains of Çiron, at Hi-Vator. Their nests are far up the rocks, in the caves among the crags and peaks."

"Çiron," the Lieutenant repeated. "And Hi-Vator . . . But Çiron is at the mountains' foot."

Rahm nodded. Through the remnants of his own smile, Rahm found himself looking into a face not smiling at all.

"Do all Çironians go about so?" Kire asked. "Are you all so peaceful? Perhaps, you, boy, are just simple-minded—"

"We are peaceful, yes. We have no guns, if that is what thou meanst. Many of us go naked—though not all."

Black cloth hanging close around, the Lieutenant chuckled.

And Rahm laughed with him, putting his feet wide and taking a great breath to support his laughter, throwing back black hair—so that he seemed to overflow the space which was naturally and generously his. "But thou art the first ever to think me simple!"

"Where are you coming from now, Çironian? Who are your parents? How do you live?"

"I come from a week's wandering, out in the land. It is our village custom that every person so wander, once every three years. My parents both died of a fever when I was a boy. Old Ienbar the gravedigger took me in, and I work with him—when there is need. At other times, I help in the grain fields."

"Those muscles are all from grave digging, hoe hefting, and plow pushing?"

"Some, yes." Rahm raised an arm to make an indifferent fist. "I always take a prize at the village games. But much comes from the year I unloaded stones with Brumer and Heben and Gargula, and Tenuk who works with me now in the fields; and the other boys on the rock crew—for our new council-building foundation!"

"And you don't even know what a weapon . . ." From the rock he'd settled against, Kire stood and turned—like a man who suddenly finds the joke empty enough simply to walk away. As he tromped back up the hill, his heavy cape, that no wind made billow or belly, moved only a bit, left and right. The mare raised her head. Kire took up the reins, grasped the saddle horn and, raising one boot to the stirrup, swung up and over.

"Friend Kire!" the Çironian called. "The lion! Wouldst thou go without my gift?"

As the mare reared and turned, Kire called back hoarsely: "I haven't forgotten." He guided the horse down the slope.

Rahm grasped a hind leg with one hand and an opposite forefoot with the other. He hefted the corpse high, its head hanging back.

The mouth was wide.

The teeth were bared.

The horse shied at the dead thing, but Kire bent down to grab a handful of loose fur. He tugged—while Rahm pushed—the puma across the horse's back. The gift in place, Kire leaned down and, with his black glove, grasped the Çironian's shoulder. "I will not forget it," and he muttered, wheeling: "though someday *you* may want to." But the last was lost in leaf chatter under the horse's hooves and the general roughness of his voice.

Hooves beat the earth—and Rahm leapt back.

Kire of Myetra gained the rise, while his cloak slid no more than from haunch to haunch on his mare's mahogony rump. With a flap of the reins, he was gone—to leave Rahm puzzled at their parting.

CHAPTER
TWO

N aä sings so prettily," said one.
"Naä sings like a bird," said another.
"Like a lark."

And between the women Rimgia bent among the rows, that, rising up over her eyes, became a gold jungle webbed with Naä's song. Rimgia wrapped her hands in the stalks and pulled. She'd been working some hours and her side was sore. In another hour the edge of her palms would sting.

But Naä sang.

And the song *was* beautiful.

Did they really work better when the singer sang? From time to time, when one could pay attention to the words, it was certainly more pleasant to work that way. Most of the women *said* they worked better. And all of the men. And it was best, Rimgia knew, not to say too much at odds with what most people said, unless you'd thought about it carefully and long—and selected your words with precision. That last had been added to the village truism by her father Kern—a man known more for his silence than his volubility.

While Rimgia picked and listened, the squeak-squeak-clunk, squeak-squeak-clunk of the water cart rose out of the breeze and the music. Rimgia stood up, to feel gas rumble in her stomach from hunger. The water cart's arrival was her signal to cease and go home.

Apparently, it was Naä's too. At the end of the verse, when the jolly man, so strong and fair, kissed the girl with the raven hair, Naä hefted her harp on its leather strap around behind her back, unhooked her left knée from her right ankle, and pushed herself down from the rock. She shook her brown hair back, hailed stocky Mantice, the water-cart driver. (His name had three syllables, the last with the softest "c." In that locale it meant a bird, not a bug.)

Receiving the smiles and warm words from the working women, Rimgia, whose hair was the color of the central length inside a split carrot, got a dipper of water from Mantice at the cart; and, laughing at one woman and whispering to another about still another's new boyfriend and giving a quick grin to another who stepped up, full of a story about someone else's four-year-old daughter, she hurried to the path to fall in beside the singer.

When she saw Rimgia coming, Naä lingered for her.

They'd walked together a whole minute,

when Rimgia asked: "Naä, what dost thou think happens to us when we die?" She asked the question because Naä was a person you could ask such things of, and she wouldn't laugh, and she wouldn't go telling other people how strange you were, and you wouldn't hear people talking and whispering about you when you came around the corner or surprised them by the well a day later.

That was more the reason for the question than that Rimgia really wanted to know. Indeed, she rather liked the idea that the wandering singer sometimes found her, and her occasional odd thoughts, of interest enough to speak about them seriously. So—sometimes—Rimgia tried to make her own thoughts seem more serious than they were.

"When we die?" Naä pondered. "I suspect it's just a big, blank nothing, forever and ever and ever, that you don't even know is there—because there is no knowing any more. That, I guess, is the safest thing to bet on, at least in terms of living your life the best you can while you're alive." She paused. "But once I was in a land—oh, three or four years back—that had the strangest ideas about that."

"Yes?" Rimgia asked. "How so?"

"The elders of its villages were convinced that there was only a single great consciousness in all the universe, a consciousness that was free to roam through all space and all time, backwards and forwards, not only over all of this world but through all the hundreds and millions and hundreds of millions of worlds, from the beginning of time to its very end. You know the little signs Ienbar makes on his bark scrolls about each person he buries, up at the burial field? Even fifty years after someone has died here, Ienbar can go to his scrolls and tell you what his name was, where she lived, who were their children, and what work and what good deeds and bad deeds were once remembered about each person in the village. Well, according to those elders, you and I are not really alive—we're not really living our lives, here and now, as we walk along the path, pushing the branches aside that grow out of the underbrush." She caught and released a branch; it whooshed back behind them. "What we think and feel and experience as our own consciousness, living through moment after moment, is really the one great consciousness reading over our lives, from our birth to our death, as if each one of us were just an entry in Ienbar's scrolls. At whatever here-and-now moment, what you're experiencing as your present awareness is just where that consciousness happens to be—what *it's* aware of as it reads you over. But that one great consciousness is the only consciousness there is, now believing it's Rimgia the grain picker, now believing it's Tenuk the plower, now believing it's Mantice the water-cart driver, now believing it's Naä the singer. While it reads you, of course, it gets wholly involved in everything that happens, in every little detail—the way you might get involved in some song I sang last evening, in the darkness when the fire's coals were almost out, when the song seems more real than the darkness around. But that one consciousness reads through the full life not only of you and me and every human being—it reads the life of every bug and beetle and gnat, of every worm and ant and newt, the life of every hen whose neck you wring for dinner and every kid whose throat you cut to roast; and of every grass blade and every flower and every tree as well. It reads through every good and friendly and helpful deed and happening. It reads through every painful, harmful, and hurtful thing that has fallen to anyone or any creature either by carelessness or conscious evil."

"But what's all this reading of all of us for?" Rimgia laughed. (Naä's notions could sometimes be odder than the questions that prompted them.) "Is it to learn something? To learn what life is about—the lives of gnats and people and flowers and hens and bugs and goats and trees?"

"That's where the theory gets rather strange," Naä explained. "What that great, single consciousness-that-is-the-here-and-now-consciousness-of-all-of-us is trying to learn is what life . . . *isn't*: the greater Life that is its own complete totality. You see, after it's finished reading you, it knows that, however important and interesting and involving the various parts of your life were, that is not *really* what Life is about. But only after it's finished reading through the whole of your life, only after it's actually become you and experienced the length of your years, can it know that, for certain. And only after it's finished reading me, does it know that my life was not the essence either. And so it goes, with every wise old hermit and every mindless mosquito and every great king who rules a nation. And when it's completely finished with all the things it could possibly read, from the life of every sickly infant dead an hour after birth to every hundred-year-old hag who finally drops into death, from every minnow eaten by a frog to every elk springing from a mountain peak and every eagle soaring above them, to every chick dead in the egg three days before it hatches, only then will it be released from its reading, to be its wondrous and glorious self, with the great and universal simplicity that it's learned. That's what those elders thought—and that's what they told their people."

The two young women walked silently.

Then Naä went on: "I must say, though I found it an interesting idea, I'm not sure I believe it. I think I'd rather take the nothing."

"Really?" Rimgia asked, surprised; for, as an idea to turn over and consider, like the petals of a black-eyed Susan, it had intrigued her. "Why?"

"Well, when I was a little girl, playing in the yard of my parents' hut in Calvicon, and I'd think about such things—death, I mean—the idea of all that nothing after my little bit of a life used to frighten me—terribly, so that my mouth would dry, my heart would hammer, and I'd sweat like I'd just run a race . . . from time to time I'd almost collapse with my fear of it; there it waited, at the end of my life, to swallow me into it. Nothing. Nothing for millions of billions of years more than the millions of billions of years that are no part at all of all the years there are. Really, when such thoughts were in my head, I couldn't sing a note! But then, a little later, when I heard this other idea, it occurred to me that, really, *it* was much more frightening! If I—and you—really are that great consciousness, and really are one, that means 'I'—the great consciousness that I am—must go through *everyone's* pain, *everyone's* agonies, *everyone's* dying and death, animal as well as human, bird and fish, beast and plant, and all the unfairness and cruelty and pain in the universe: not only yours and mine, but the pain of every bug anyone ever squashed and every worm that comes out of the ground in the rain to dry up on a rock." Naä chuckled. "Well, it's all I can do to get through my own life. I mean, doesn't it sound *exhausting*?"

They walked in the dust a while. Finally Rimgia said (because this was something she had thought about many times before): "I wish I could change places with thee, Naä—could just put my feet into the prints thy feet leave on the path and from there go where thou goest, see what thou seest. I wish I could become thee! And give up being me."

"Whatever for?" Naä knew how much the youngsters were in awe of her; but, whenever it came out in some open way, it still surprised her.

"Once every three years," Rimgia said, "I'll go on a wander for a week—maybe tramp far enough to find a village so much like Çiron that I might as well not have started out. Or I'll sit in the woods and dream. And the most exciting thing that'll actually happen will be that I see a Winged One from Hi-Vator pass overhead. But thou hast been to dozens of lands, Naä. And thou wilt go to dozens more. Thou hast learned the songs of peoples all over the world and thou hast come to sing them here to us—and thou makest us, for the moments of thy song, soar like men and women with wings—while all I do is go home from the fields to cook for my brother and father." She laughed a little, because she was a good girl, who loved her father and brother even as she complained of them. "So now thou knowst why, for a while at any rate, I would be thee!"

"Well," Naä said, "I must cook for myself—and though most days I like it, some days are lonely. Nor is the lean-to I live in all that comfortable." Even saying it, Naä was thinking that she wouldn't change her life with a king's. For the friendly, gregarious, and curious folk of Çiron made real loneliness a difficult state to maintain. "Right now, though, I've got to see Ienbar in his shack at the burial meadow. I told him I would come by today, once the water cart passed. But I shall see you tomorrow—and, who knows, maybe make a song about a wonderfully interesting red-headed woman who, while she cooks for her brother and father, takes her questions to . . . the very edge of death and back!"

"Thou'rt the one going to the burial field," Rimgia said, pretending not to be desperately pleased at the prospect of being the subject of a song. "And thou'rt the one who has heard all the strange ideas of the world—not I. Yes, I would change places with thee, if I could, Naä—though if those foreign elders' strange idea is right, it means that I may *have* to live your life, and you mine, someday—that we might change places yet!"

"Or that we already have," Naä said. "In fact

that's one reason, I guess, I have trouble with it. But, when I see you tomorrow, I'll tell you what Ienbar says. That's next best to going to see him, isn't it?"

"And some time soon thou must come and eat with us. And sing this new song for Abrid and my father—Father likes thy singing almost as much as I do."

And, laughing, the two women parted to go their different ways through the town.

When he reached the first field, Rahm paused to fill his chest with the scent of grain under hot sun and to listen to the roar of crickets, to grass spears brushing one another, and to sparrows and crows and jays which all, with another breath, would again become what, at any other time, he would think of as silence.

Halfway across the field, Tenuk the plower looked up, halted his animal, and waved. Ahead of the plow, the mule was the hue of cut slate. A distant ear twitched—and, waving back, Rahm imagined the rasping blue-bottle worrying at the eyelashes of that diligent, tractable beast.

With more humor than reproach, Rahm thought: Tenuk's only three days further along than when I left . . . They've missed me here.

Beets grew to Rahm's right. Kale stretched to his left. He walked along one field's edge. The earth was soft. Yellowing grasses brushed and itched his sweating calves. Moist soil gave and sprang back to his bare soles. Even as he tried to take in all that was familiar about his fields, his country, his home, one new bit of the familiar was wiped away with the next.

He turned onto the path toward town. Moments later, trotting out under lowering oak branches, he saw the woman at the stone-walled well halt, clay jug at her hip; she recognized him—and smiled. Rahm grinned back, as four children careened from behind the door-hanging of the hut across the way, a dog yipping among them. (Three years ago and a head-and-a-half shorter, in her dirty hands the oldest of those children had held that dog up to him as a puppy, and Rahm had said, "Why not call him 'Mouse'? A big mouse—that's what he looks like," and the girl and the others had laughed, because it was such a silly idea—calling a dog a mouse!) They ran toward him, not seeing him. As they broke around him, he caught up the youngest and swung her to his shoulder as she squealed. And suddenly he was among them, the others jumping around him and clapping. The little one grappled his long hair, and her squeal became laughter that, somewhere in it, had his name. And he said all theirs, and their mothers', and their fathers', then theirs again ("Hello, Jallet. Hey there, Wraga . . . How is thy mother, Kenisa? Jallet, dost thy fat old man Mantice still waste his time with the water cart . . . ? I did not see thy uncle Gargula in the fields today. Perhaps he's still doing some work for thy mother? But thou must not let Veema work him too hard, Nugo! Tell her I told you so, too! Let Gargula get back to the beet fields, where he's needed! Wraga, so long . . ."), and called them all out again in farewell, because it pleased him—almost surprised him—that, after a week in the wild, those names that he had not thought of

over all the adventurous days, names that he
might as well have forgotten, came back so
quickly to his tongue. A step more, and he set
the little girl down. She grabbed hold of his
forefinger, now, tugging and calling for another ride. But Rahm laughed and freed himself. And they were running on.

Where she'd carried her loom out into her
yard, to sit cross-legged on the ground, Hara
looked up from her strings and shuttles and
separator plank and tamping paddle. A breeze
lifted the ends of the leaf-green rag tied around
hair through which white flowed like currents
in a stream; it moved the hem of her brown
skirt back from browner ankles. Her breasts
were flat and long, the aureoles wide around
dark dugs. Her eyes were black and glittering
within their clutch of wrinkles—that deepened
when she saw him. "Hello to thee, young
Rahm!"

Rahm came over, to stand behind her and
look down. Crouching now, he frowned at her
pattern: blue, orange, green, cut away sharply
by the unwoven strings. "What makest thou
there?"

"Who knows," Hara said, her smile more full
of spaces than teeth. "Perhaps it's something
thou mayest wear thyself one day, when they
decide in the council house that a bit of
youth's foolishness has gone out of thee and
more of the world's wisdom has settled between thy ears."

That made Rahm laugh. He patted the
weaver's shoulder—and stood, still able to feel
where the girl, gone now, had sat on his.

Hara slammed down the treadle. The shuttle

ran through quivering threads, drawing gray yarn.

Rahm loped off between stone and thatch buildings. Toward him from an alley end, an ox lugged a creaking cart. The side slats were woven with wide leather strips, the bed piled with rocks.

Its two drivers, man and boy, were gray from cracked, callused toes to bushy beard (on the elder) and hair. The man raised an arm to Rahm, even as he frowned—as though the rock dust powdering his face and beard made a fog hard to see through. But the boy, who held a sack on his lap, suddenly pushed it to the bench, stood in his seat, and called out: "Rahm!"

Stopping, Rahm grinned. "Hey, Abrid—!"

Washed free of quarry powder, Kern's hair and beard would be the same powder gray. But after a splash from the bucket, Abrid's braids would be as red as his sister's. And because I know that, thought Rahm, that's how I know I'm home!

Kern halted the cart with a grunt. His frown deepened. He nodded to Rahm. But Kern's frown was as welcoming, Rahm knew, as any smile.

Abrid jumped down from the bench and seized Rahm's wrist the way a much younger child might, though the grit on his palms made the boy's hand feel like an old man's. "You will work again with us at the stone pits, Rahm?"

"No, Abrid." Rahm shook his head. "I will stay in the fields—"

* * *

Inside the house Rimgia had put the dough cakes on the hot stones down at the fire and was tossing handfuls of cut turnips and sliced squash and chopped radishes into the bowl of lettuces she had torn up, when something in the voices outside caught her. She turned from the counter and stepped across the floor mat— she needed more water. As she went, she hooked two fingers in the handle of the jar sitting there; but it was already half full. Holding the jar, she pulled in the door with the other hand and stepped out onto the porch over the high sill (which kept the heavy winter rains from coming up to the door—Abrid better fix that loose plank soon). She looked out, to call: "Father, Abrid, come in and get your—!"

Her father, Kern, still sitting on the cart seat, and her brother, Abrid, already standing, looked around.

She saw Rahm.

Reaching up to run her hand, still moist from the water in which she'd washed the vegetables, across her forehead and into her hair, Rimgia set the water pitcher on the porch planks and, with a surge of delight, rushed barefoot down the steps. "Rahm! Thou wilt stay to eat with us . . . ?" Again a hand to her hair to brush back some from her forehead (yes, Rahm thought, the same red as her brother's beneath his work-dust); but her face was full of a smile that wanted to get even bigger, wanted to swallow all the sunlight and breeze around them. She wiped her other hand on her shift's hip. "Come, stay—there's more than enough! And thou canst tell us of all thy adventures in thy wander. Did you get back this morning? Or last night—?"

"I only tramped in by the southern fields ten minutes past, and glimpsed Tenuk—stalking his mule. I'll come and see thee soon, Rimgia. But I haven't even told Ienbar I'm here."

Abrid jumped down and came around the cart—he almost bumped the corner, but swung his hip away—to stand near the steps. He lifted the pitcher, frowned into it, then poured some into his hand. He splashed his face, threw another handful against his chest. Water fell to darken the dust on one knee, the toes of one foot. Sitting on the step now, with two fingers together, he wiped his light lashes free of dirt. "Hey, *why* wilt thou not stay, Rahm?"

"I will, but some other time, boy!"

"Well, then." Rimgia went to the cart bench to take down the sack Abrid had left on the seat. (In it, Rahm knew, would be pears—and some melons—Abrid had gathered from the orchards up near the quarry. Yes, he was home.) As she did so, the scent of the baked dough cakes came from the door. Rahm smiled—and Rimgia wondered if the scent was what he smiled at. (How many dozens of them had she seen Rahm, now sitting on the well wall, now walking across the commons, wolf down in the last year—?) "Then thou must come back soon."

Climbing from the wagon beside her, her father turned and clapped Rahm's shoulder. And still frowned, silently—but silence was Kern's way.

Rahm said: "When I've seen Ienbar, I'll return."

"Thou mayest see Naä there," Rimgia said. "Earlier, when I came with her from the fields, she too was off to talk with him." These people here, my brother, my father, and Rahm (Rimgia thought), perhaps we *are* all a single consciousness and only believe ourselves separate, so that we are closest to the truth at a moment like this when we almost forget it. The notion, odd as it was, made her smile even more than the pleasure of her friend's return.

And with all the smiling and nodding and grinning and waving—that seemed the only comfortable thing to do (or frowning, if you were Kern) when you'd been away and come back—Rahm left his friends and their father.

There was another young man in that village, who, though he had lost his parents during the same autumnal fever that had killed Rahm's almost a decade ago, was as different from Rahm as a young man could be—for, though likely he loved it as much, he had a very different view of Çiron.

Qualt hauled a great basket of yellow rinds and chicken feathers and milkslops and egg shells and corn shucks from his wagon, to go, stiff-legged and leaning back against it, over the mossy stones to overturn it, rushing and bouncing down, at the ravine precipice into the soggy and steaming gully. A lithe and wiry youngster of twenty-two, given to bursts of intense conversation, long periods of introspection, and occasional smiles that startled his face but would linger there half a morning, he was the town garbage collector.

And Qualt was in love with red-haired Rimgia.

Qualt stood at the rocky rim, the empty basket in his big hands. (Unlike Rahm, Qualt's hands—and feet—were the only things you might call big about him; oh, yes, and perhaps his ears, if his hair was tied back—though it wasn't now. Really, he was a rather slight young fellow.) Qualt breathed slowly, not smelling, really, what lay among the rocks below.

A few weeks before, you see, when a number of Çiron's young people, Qualt, Rimgia, Abrid, and Rahm among them, had gone for a full-moon swim at the quarry lake, they'd all sung songs (Rahm the loudest, Qualt the best), most of them learned from Naä, and cooked sweet-dough on sticks over the open fire (the way Ienbar had suggested they try) till very late, and finally gone chastely to sleep. Qualt and Rimgia had slept, yes, on the same blanket: Qualt's blanket. Yes, Rimgia and Qualt—head to heel, heel to head—the water a silver sheet beside them. Qualt had woken, just at dawn and a bit before the others, to find Rimgia's arm over his calf and her cheek pressed against his callused ball and wide toes. Her eyes had been closed and her breath had made the tiniest whistle he'd almost not heard for the sound of the current, the splash of small fish, and the morning's first birds. But he'd lain, staring down over his hip, afraid to move lest she wake, his heart hammering harder and harder, so that it was all he could do to pay attention to the feel of—yes, he could move them without disturbing her—the toes on his right foot in the copper torrent, the cataract, the cool swirl of her hair.

Later, he'd decided she was a strange girl. But when, in all the nights between then and today, he'd drifted off to sleep, he kept finding a dark tenderness among his thoughts of her.

Suddenly Qualt smacked the basket bottom, turned it up to peer within its smelly slats, then dragged it behind him, rasping on rock, toward the dozen others that stood around the end of his wagon.

Rahm walked through the village, wondering at how well he knew his home's morning-to-morning and evening-to-evening cycle.

In hours, Rahm thought, the sun will drop behind the trees, and the western houses will unroll shadows over the streets. Then, at dawn, the sun will push between the eastern dwellings to stripe the dust with copper. He strolled on, hugely content.

Reaching the burial meadow, Rahm glanced over the unmarked graves. (But Ienbar knew the name and location of each man, each woman, and each child laid here time out of memory, and kept all the scrolls about them. . . .) The visiting singer was coming toward the meadow up the road from the fields.

A chamois mantle hung forward over one shoulder but was pushed back from the other. A chain of shells held her short skirt low on her hips. A strap ran down between her breasts, holding something to her back. Its carved wooden head slanted behind her neck. Rahm knew it was her harp. "And hello to thee, Naä."

"Rahm, you're back! Are you going to see Ienbar? I was on my way to visit him, but I stopped at my lean-to to replace three of my harp-strings—"

"Yes, Rimgia told me, only moments past," Rahm said. "Kern and Abrid were just home from the stone pits."

"And in your wander, what'd you see?" She fell in beside him. "That's what I want to hear about!"

"Naä—" Rahm looked at the ground, where olive tufts poked from the path dust—"thou makest fun of me."

"What do you mean, make fun?"

"Thou, who hast traveled over all the world, asketh me what I have seen that thou hast not, after a simple week's wander . . . ?"

"Oh, Rahm—I wasn't making fun of you. I'm interested!"

"But thou hast come all the way from Calvicon, with thy songs and tales. What can I have seen in a week that thou in a dozen years hast not?"

"But that's what I want you to tell me!"

He saw her glance over to catch his expression (he was still pretending interest in the tufted ridge of the path)—and saw her surprise that his expression was a smile. "But now thou seest," he said, looking at her again, "I am making fun of *thee!*"

"We'll go to Ienbar together, and while we go, you'll tell me!"

"Naä, I saw antelopes come down across hazed-over grasses to drink at yellow watering holes at dawn. I found a village of folk who wove and plowed and quarried as we do, and live in huts and houses that might well have been built on the same plans as ours—though the only words in the whole of their language I could make out, after a day with them, were the words for 'star,' 'ear,' and 'tomato plant.' On the fifth day, as the rituals instruct us, I ate nothing from the time I woke, but drank only water, and stopped three times to purify myself with wisewords. And, when the sun went down, still fasting I composed myself for sleep—hoping for a mystic dream."

She grinned: "Did you have one?"

"I dreamt," Rahm said, gravely, "that I walked by a great, rushing stream. And as the sun rose up, and I ambled along beside the current, the water began to sparkle. Then, in the dream, a little branch feeding into the water lay before me, so I decided to wade across to the other side. I stepped in. The water was cold at first—but a few steps on, as the water reached my thighs and finally my waist, it grew warm. Then, even warmer. And warmer. I woke—" He chuckled—"to find I had pissed myself, the way I used to when I was a boy in bed, a couple of times a week, even unto my fifteenth year— and my mother would become angry and say I made the shack stink." The chuckle became a laugh. "Then she'd make me go sleep out in the tool cabin. But that, I'm afraid, was all there was of mystic dreaming!"

"Oh, Rahm—well, you'd better not tell Ienbar that." Naä laughed outright. "Then again, maybe you should. He just might find something in it—if he just doesn't find it funny, too."

"Then I found a very real, very un-mystic—"

Rahm laughed again—"stream and washed myself; and went on my way. And this morning," he finished, "I was attacked by a wild prairie lion and wrestled with her, to break her neck with my arm. Then I came home here."

Naä shook her head. "Rahm, you folk amaze me."

He looked at her as they walked, his amber eyes full of questioning.

"Three months ago, when I first came here, I'd never have believed such people as you existed." Naä paused a moment, as if searching within for her answer. "Sometimes, I still don't believe that you do."

"Why, Naä?"

"Rahm, I've traveled to lots of places, through lots of lands. I know songs and stories from even more lands and places than I've visited—more lands and places than you could imagine. But most of the songs and stories I know are about fights and wars, about love that dies, about death and betrayal and revenge. Yet here there is . . ." She raised her shoulders, and looked up at the branches whose early summer green had begun to go smoky after the first bright hue of spring. "But I can't even name it." She let her shoulders fall. "Here, I go out and sing to Rimgia and to the other women in the fields. I come and exchange songs and tales with Ienbar, or go sit and talk with Hara over her shuttles. Sometimes I eat with you in the evening, or take long walks alone in the foothills of the mountains. If any woman of the village comes around a corner of the path, my heart leaps as happily as if it were my own sister coming to meet me. If any

man of the village crosses my path, we smile
and call to each other with the same warmth I'd
call to my own brother." She glanced at him,
then glanced away. "Whenever a group of you
get together, after work in the evening, or
before a council meeting, and everyone turns
to me and asks me to sing . . . well, I've never
sung better!" Naä looked down at the dust.
"The only thing any of you say there is to fear
in the whole of this land are the flying creatures from Hi-Vator. And no one can even remember why that is—so even that's awfully
easy to forget; and since I've been here, I've
only once seen what might have been a silhouette of one against some moonshot clouds,
anyway.

"Rahm, the last time I was in my own father's
hut in Calvicon, when I and my four brothers
and my sister were all together, it was when my
stepmother, who had been so good to us once
my real mother died, was so ill. We sat around,
with my father, beside my stepmother's sick-
bed, talking together about our childhood. And
how joyful and wonderful and loving and free it
had been, because of him, because of her. And
as we sat there, talking softly and laughing
quietly in the firelight, I kept thinking, '*Nobody* has a childhood as wonderful as we're
now all saying we did. *I* certainly didn't.' For,
like any other parents, however much they
loved us, often they had been bored with us,
and sometimes they slapped us, and now and
again they were sullen and angry that we
weren't interested in the things that concerned them—while they were wholly oblivious to what we felt was so important. Yet we

all—my brothers, my sister, and me, too—went
on talking about that time as if the moments of
love and concern, my stepmother's smile at a
chipmunk my youngest brother caught for a
pet, the corn cakes my father baked for a friend
of mine's party when I asked him, or the songs
the two of them sang together once, just after
dark by our bedside, had been, indeed, the
whole of it. And while the flames fell back into
the embers, it struck me: This isn't a story of
some real childhood that we're telling of now.
No, this story is a present we're making for my
worried old father and my sick, sick stepmother, for having been two very, very fine parents indeed—and who'd certainly given us a
childhood fine *enough*. But once I realized
what sort of present it was, I was happy to sit
there for another hour, completing that present, weaving it together with my brothers and
sister—I was happy to make it for them, happy
to give it to them; and I went to sleep after-
wards, content we'd done it. And three days
later, I left on another journey, knowing I
would never see that fine old woman again, and
that there was a good chance I might not ever
see my father again either—but thinking no
more about the story we'd given them, those
few nights ago, than anyone ever thinks about
a present you've given gladly to someone who
deserves it." Naä was silent a few steps more.
"At least I didn't think about it until after I'd
been here, oh, three weeks or a month. Because, you see, Rahm, you've all, here, given a
present to me.

"You've given me—not another childhood;

but rather a time like the *story* of childhood we put together that evening to help my parents through their final years. And, till now, I wouldn't have believed a time or a place like that was possible!" They walked on together over the warm earth. "It's beautiful here, Rahm. So beautiful that if I were anywhere else and tried to sing of this beauty, the notes would stick in my throat, the words would stall on my tongue—and I'd start to cry."

They had reached a stretch of green graves and stopped to gaze at where stone slanted from the smoky grass. "Yes," Rahm said, after a moment. "It is beautiful, Naä. Thou art right."

Naä took a long, long breath. "So you brought a puma back with you. Did you leave it down with Kern and Rimgia? I wonder what sort of stew Ienbar will make out of *that*— before he puts the claws on his necklace."

"I didn't bring it back," Rahm said. "I gave it to a friend."

"You gave it to someone in the village before you brought it to show Ienbar?" She laughed. "Now that's the first thing I think you've ever done that's shocked me!"

"Not a friend in the village. This was a man who helped me on my journey. As I fought the cat, a Winged One flew close. This man frightened it away with a powergun."

Naä turned to look at him. "A powergun? In my home, Calvicon, a man came through once with a powergun. He used it to do scary tricks—set a bushel of hay on fire—in the market square. But he told my big brother, who was his friend for a while, that they could be really dangerous, if used improperly . . . Where was he from?"

Rahm shrugged. "He wore a black cloak. And black gloves. And a black hood. There was a silver crow on his shoulder—and on the sling which held his gun. His name was Kire, and I—"

"Myetra . . ." Naä's face darkened.

"Possibly," Rahm said. "But why dost thou look so strangely at this."

"Crow, cloak, and hood, in black and silver, are the uniform of officers in the Myetran army. What would such a soldier be doing here—so close you could leave him in the morning and be here by noon?" She walked, considering. "And with a powergun. Were there others with him?"

"I saw only the one alone. He said he was a wanderer like me, out to see our land."

"—with a powergun? It doesn't sound good at all."

"By why, Naä? We do not know them."

"Calvicon knows them," she said. "And what they know isn't good. We'd better tell Ienbar, anyway."

They had reached the center of the field.

"If he is at home." Rahm looked around. He cupped his hands to shout. "Ienbar, I am here! Where art thou?"

On the meadow's far side, a door in a board wall between two trees flew open. A figure lurched out. White hair and white beard jutted in small braids. "Rahm!" the old man shouted and began to rush bandy-legged across the grass. Round his neck jangled half a dozen

thongs tied with animal teeth. His long arms
were heavy with copper bracelets. At his waist,
a leather apron was hemmed with metal pieces
worked with symbols and designs. Metal circled his ankle above a skinny foot. Several
huge brass hoops hung from his ears, their
thickness distending pierced lobe and rim.

Ienbar threw his clinking arms around
Rahm, stepped back, then embraced him
again. "My son!" he said, in a voice cracked
and crackling, then stepped back, while Rahm
steadied his scrawny shoulders in his big
hands. "Thou hast come safely from thy wandering." Turning to Naä, the old man seized
her wrist. "And thou hast come too, my daughter, to sing and play for me. It is good to see
thee this fine day."

"It's always good to see you, Ienbar," Naä
said. "Just like it's good to have Rahm back
with us."

"Come, the both of you," Ienbar declared.
"Well, boy, where hast thou been and what
didst thou see?"

In the hut, they sat on mats Rahm tossed
across small benches, while Ienbar heated his
pot. Shelves about them were stacked with
bones and parchment scrolls, bits of beautiful
uncut stone, lengths of painted wood, dried liz-
ards, stuffed bats, and the mounted skeletons
of various ground birds and field creatures.
Some of the village children still entered here
with fear—but to Rahm it had been his home
since the death of his parents when he was fifteen.

". . . what a dream!" Ienbar chuckled. "What
a dream, indeed! Yes, I recall that river, from

the first years thou hadst moved in with me here, I do—" Ienbar grinned at a reproving look from Rahm. "Well, I do! Sometimes, I think, thy sleeping corner still smells of it—and I've told thee before, I don't mind. I rather like it. A bit of dung, a bit of urine, fresh turned earth, and new cut grass—those are good smells!" Ienbar broke a small bone and, on the pot's rim, tapped the marrow into the broth. "The smells I don't like, now—charred meat, rotten vegetables, and the stench of clogged water that should be running free." Ienbar turned to serve Naä, then Rahm; for himself, at last, he filled a third bowl. "Well, well, what a dream, what a stream . . . !"

Rahm took one sip; then, bowl between his knees, he began on the rest of his wander. But when he reached the encounter with the Myetran, the old man's face wrinkled.

Ienbar put his soup on the hearth-flags by his big-knuckled toes with their thickened nails, sat back, and moved his tongue about in his mouth without opening his lips.

Questioningly, Rahm lowered black brows. "Why art thou and Naä so concerned about these Myetrans?"

Ienbar sucked his gums. "Oh, sometimes one hears stories—"

Naä interrupted: "I'll tell you a story, Rahm—" She looked across her bowl at the old man. "Ienbar—in Calvicon, we hear stories too. And the stories of Myetra were never good. I told you about my brother's friend, Rahm? Well, he said that his powergun was from Myetra. And he told stories of the destruction that went on there—between man and man, be-

tween one race and another. You have your flying neighbors at Hi-Vator? Well, Myetra is on
the sea—and once there were people who lived
and swam in the water, and could breathe
under it like fish do in the ponds and the
stream in the quarry. But Myetra fought them;
and made slaves of them; and finally killed
them. And there are no more water folk around
the Myetran shore. That's the story my
brother's friend told us. Then, one day, long
after he had told us this, my brother's friend
disappeared—and the tale that came back was
that he and another man had gotten angry at
one another, gotten into a fight, and finally my
brother's friend had used the powergun to kill
him. He disappeared the next day, and we
never saw him again."

"To *kill* . . . ?" Rahm asked.

"Yes, there have been stories of such things
before." Ienbar nodded.

"To frighten a Winged One, yes. But why to
kill—and another man? Human beings do not
kill each other. Thou killest a goat to roast
it, an ox to butcher it. But not a human being . . ."

"If they come by here," Ienbar said, "we
must keep out of their way—"

"But this did not seem to be a brutal man
that I met—not a man who would kill. He frightened away the Winged One. He spoke to me as
to a friend."

"That is a good sign, I suppose. Perhaps
there's nothing to fear." Ienbar shrugged,
clinking, to pick up his bowl and stare across
it at the flames that, because of the open window, were so diminished by the Çironian sun.

"Perhaps . . . after all, it is only a single soldier wandering through the country—"

"I think that's what he was," Rahm said, and raised his bowl to drink. "Yes," he said between sips. "That is what he was."

"I hope you're right," Naä said, less confidently. Then she swung the harp to her lap to pluck a run on the lower strings.

CHAPTER
THREE

———◆———

Rahm slept deeply, one hand low on his belly. His lids showed white crescents between black lashes. Outside the shack the air cooled. For a while, despite the warmth, it seemed a light rain might come; but at last, without a drop's falling, the moon's curve came out, as thin as what showed of Rahm's eyes.

The clouds moved away, and the night air dried in the newmoon light as if it had been full sun.

Then sound jabbed into sleep.

It grew till it ripped sleep apart—and Rahm sat upright, to smash his hands' heels against his head, then again, trying to find his ears to cover them ... against something he could not, for this moment, distinguish between pain and sound.

Ienbar leaned against the fireplace, shaking, his mouth opening, closing. His arm flailed about—but the clinking of his bracelets was lost in the wailing that filled Rahm's ears with pressure enough to burst them.

Rahm lurched to his feet and staggered to the door, pulling it open. The sound—because it *was* a sound—came from across the village. As Rahm stepped outside, it became a booming voice:

SURRENDER, PEOPLE OF ÇIRON!
SURRENDER TO THE FORCES OF MYETRA!

Then silence.
The absence of sound stung Rahm's ears.
He tried to blink the water out of his eyes.
The wailing began again. Anticipating pain, Rahm stepped back into the doorway as the voice churned through the darkness:

PEOPLE OF ÇIRON!
SURRENDER TO THE FORCES OF MYETRA!

Behind him, Ienbar was crying.
Rahm sprinted out onto the path, shaking his head to clear it while he ran, to throw off the pain and the steady high hum, loud as any roaring, that covered all else. Leaves pulled away, and the village lights flickered. As he passed the first houses, he heard distraught voices. Certainly, no villager still slept!

To the east, light flared. Then another flare. Another. Three lights fanned the dark, lowering, till they struck—blindingly—among the huts.

Rahm's first panicked thought was that the shacks would burst into fire under the glare. But apparently the lights were for illumination—or for the terror such illumination in the midst of darkness might bring.

Rahm's hearing had almost returned to normal.

Somewhere drums thudded.

Naä dreamed she had stumbled into her harp. Only it was huge. And as she tried to fight through the strings, they began to ring and sing and siren—they were all around her, her arms and head and legs, till the harp itself broke—and she woke, pulling herself out of her sleeping blankets and scrambling from under the lean-to's edge, disoriented at the incredible sound.

Qualt had his own house, but slept outside that night with his back against his wagon's wheel, because the weather was warm and the night was easy.

We won't say that, as he lay there, breathing across his large, loose fingers, relaxed before his face, he was actually dreaming of Rimgia. But when, earlier that night, he'd first lain down on this blanket to stretch out beside his garbage wagon, certainly he'd been thinking of her.

For recently sleep had become an entrance into that part of him that was becoming aware that the shape and limit of his tenderness toward her could only be learned from the thought of her hand in his hands, his face against her belly, her lap against his cheek, his mouth against her neck. So when, later, the noise came, sirening in the dark, it tore him out of something comforting as a good dream—yet without sound or image or idea to it, as dreams have.

Qualt woke, the sound around his head a solid thing. He rocked back, buttock banging the cart wheel. His hand went off the blanket, into grass and gravel. Scrabbling to sit, then to stand, he looked around the darkness. Gauzy light was cut off sharply by the familiar roof of his shack and two trees, rendered wholly strange. He took five steps, stopped—

Then something ahead of him and above darkened the light, the sky—where was it? And how huge was it, and what—but before he could ask what it was, it struck him. Hard. And he threw his arms around it, embracing it to keep from falling. And, with it, he fell. It was flapping and huge, smelled and moved like a live thing, and was—as he pushed one hand out—surrounded on both sides by a vast, taut membrane, that suddenly ceased to be taut as he struggled in it. Flailing on the ground, in the dark and that single-note scream filling every crevice of the night (but which came neither from him nor from whatever he struggled with), Qualt had two simultaneous impressions. First was that he'd stumbled into someone else, the two of them had fallen on the ground, and now were rolling together. The second was that some astonishing beast, with a pelt and an animal scent, was covering him like a puma leapt down at him from a roof or the sky, to fight with him there by his garbage cart—though so far, Qualt realized, he'd been neither bitten nor clawed.

Then the sound stopped—the chattering of twigs and leaves and small stones, because of his ears' ringing, seemed to Qualt to make their noise now not beneath the two of them, but rather off in some ringing metal pan.

The arms of the thing he fought—for it had arms—suddenly seized him—held him; restrained him. Qualt grasped it back. Distantly, he heard a breathing that, for a moment, he could not tell whether it was his or this other's. Then he felt himself go limp, because suddenly that was easier to do than to keep fighting in the black. Then, a voice that was not like any Qualt had ever heard before, because it seemed like a child's, high and breathy, said into his ear, only inches away, at the same time as Qualt scented the breath of a man who had been eating wild onions, so that, if anything, Qualt suddenly felt something familiar in all this strangeness and struggle—because Qualt himself had often walked through the lower mountains, munching the wild onion stalks that grew there:

"Hi-Vator, yes—No! Pwew! Çiron, you—?"

Rimgia dreamed that somebody, laughing hysterically, thrust a pole into her ear and out the other side of her head, then lifted her by it high into the air, over the glittering stream and she was afraid she would fall in, only it really hurt to have a pole that deep in your ear—

The pole cracked. She screamed. But before she could fall, she woke in the hut, to that in-

credible sound. Her father, Kern, was already
striding about—she saw his shape pass darkly
before the hearth embers. Pushing up quickly,
a moment later she knelt at Abrid's pallet,
shaking him.

"What is it—ow! What—?"

"Come on," she insisted, surprised when
she could not hear her own voice for the whin-
ing. "Come on!" she shouted, only realizing it
was a shout from the feel in her throat. Kern
had already opened the door, rushed out—

Rahm neared the common, where men and
women had begun to gather. As he sprinted up
the side street, someone grabbed his arm,
spun him back, hissed: "Rahm . . . !" Then:
"Where is Ienbar?"

Bewildered, he stepped back.

"For God's sake, Rahm! Where's Ienbar?"

"Naä? He's . . . at the burial meadow."

"Rahm. We have to leave—all of us. Right
now!"

"Leave? But why?"

"The Myetrans are coming! Didn't you hear
them? They want you to surrender."

"I heard. Naä, what does this 'surrender'
mean—"

"Oh, Rahm . . . !" Then, suddenly, she was
running away into the dark.

Puzzled, Rahm turned back to the gathering
in the common.

A few people still dug forefingers in their ears.
The drums were louder. From the eastern
fields another light struck. Something—a long
line of somethings—was moving toward the

common. The sweeping beams threw shadows over the beets, the grain, the kale, all bending in the night wind.

Children and mothers and uncles and cousins looked at one another.

"Why do they come across the field? They'll damage the harvest."

"There are so many of them that they couldn't fit on the road."

"Such late visitors—and so many. Will we have food for them all? They walk so strangely . . ."

Grain stalks snapped under the boots in time to the drums. As searchlights swung away, in the inadequate light from the nail paring of a moon, straining to see among the armored figures, Rahm thought to look for his friend from the morning—and, there, thought he saw him: only a moment later, he saw another tall, cloaked figure. Then another. Among the armed men advancing, a number wore the uniform Kire had worn. Some rode nervous horses; others came on foot. Their capes, despite the wind, hung straight behind them, heavy as night. Above them all, on rolling towers, the searchlights moved forward.

With the others, Rahm waited in the square.

Soon, with their mobile light-towers, the soldiers had marched to the common's near edge. The ground was fully lit. Villagers squinted. On a horse stepping about before the visitors, a bearded man in brown leather, wearing a single glove, barked at the short silver rod in his bare hand:

HALT!

Everyone looked up, because the word echoed and re-echoed from the black horns high on the moving light towers. The soldiers stopped marching. The drums stilled.

The man with the silver rod rode forward. The villagers fell back. The man spoke again. Again his voice was doubled, like thunder, from the horns:

SURRENDER TO THE FORCES OF MYETRA!

Around Rahm, people looked at one another, puzzled.

Then Kern, the quarryman, who was not really shy—only very quiet—stepped forward.

"Welcome to you . . ." he said, uncertainly. Then, which was almost twice as much as Kern ever said, he added: "Welcome, visitors in the night."

"Are you the leader here?" the mounted man demanded.

Kern didn't answer—because, as Rahm knew, Kern wasn't anyone's leader. (He was not even an elder—none of whom, Rahm noticed, seemed to have arrived yet.) Kern frowned back at the villagers behind him.

Someone called out:

"No—he's not!"

Which made a dozen people—including Rahm—laugh. Rahm whispered to Mantice who was standing beside him, "That's Tenuk," though stocky Mantice knew it was plowman Tenuk being funny as much as Rahm did. They both grinned.

"You speak for the people here," the mounted man said, which was funny in itself because Kern probably wouldn't say anything more now. But the man spoke as though he'd heard neither Tenuk's "No" nor the laughter. "You are the leader!" While his horse stepped about, he pushed the silver rod into his shirt, reached down, unfastened his sling, and lifted out his powergun—for a moment it seemed he was going to hand it to Kern as a gift.

Rahm had seen a powergun that morning, but not—really—what it could do.

Flame shot out and smacked Kern just below his shoulder. Kern slammed backward four feet—without either stepping or falling: upright, his feet just slid back across the grass—the left one was even slightly off the ground. Blood fountained a dozen feet forward. The horse's flank was splattered and the animal reared twice, then a third time. Rahm was close enough to hear the meat on Kern's chest bubble and hiss, as he fell, twisting to the side. One of Kern's arms was gone.

When it hit the ground, Kern's remaining hand moved in the grass. Kern's heavy fingers opened, then closed, with not even grass blades in them. Kern's face was gone too—and half Kern's head.

The bearded man lowered the powergun from where the retort had jerked the barrel into the air. "Your leader has been killed. So will you all be killed—unless you announce your surrender!"

Rahm felt a vast and puzzling absence inside him. Nothing in it seemed like any sort of sense he could hold to. Then, something began to grow in that senseless absence. It grew slowly. But he felt it growing. At the same

time, something—a strange understanding—
began to grow in the face of the bearded man
on his horse, who raised his gun overhead.

Suddenly the man turned sharply in his saddle and barked back at the troops:

"They refuse to surrender! Attack!"

Though he had learned far back to fight well,
like many big men Uk did not like fighting. Uncountable campaigns ago, he'd also learned
that little Mrowky actually gloried in the in-
sult, the attack, the pummeling given and received, the recovery, the re-attack. Mrowky
could make as much conversational jollity at
losing in a melée as he could at winning.

Since men—and sometimes women—so of-
ten feel obliged to start fights with big men, Uk
had grown grateful for Mrowky's willingness,
even eagerness, to jump in, when others, to
prove themselves, picked quarrels with him in
strange towns and taverns. Since people
tended not to start fights with runty men like
Mrowky (who enjoyed the fight so much),
hanging out with broad-shouldered, beer-
bellied Uk was a way to guarantee a certain fre-
quency of entertainment—possibly it was the
core of their friendship. For both were different
enough from one another to preclude close
feelings in any situation other than war.

Uk had an expansive, gentle humor he used
largely to mask from his fellows a real range of
information and some thoughtful specula-
tion—while Mrowky was, in simple words, a
loud, little, stupid man, who'd been called and
cursed by just those words enough times by
enough people so that, if he did not actually

believe they were true, he knew there was *something* to them. Thus the friendship of the big soldier, who was also smart, flattered Mrowky. Both could complain about one another in fiery terms, starred with scatology and muddied with proto-religious blasphemies.

But they were devoted.

Perhaps a little of that devotion came from the knowledge both shared, that their time in the Myetran army had taught them: life in the midst of battle was on another plane entirely from that in which relationships could be parsed (a concept Uk would understand) or parceled out (an idea Mrowky might follow), analyzed, or made rational.

With ten other soldiers, Mrowky and Uk had been stationed just along the turn-off at the common's south corner. (Other units of a dozen each had been deployed at seven more points around the green.) When the first villagers hurried by, still unsteady from the grating whine of the high speakers and more or less oblivious to the soldiers (basically because they were just not used to seeing soldiers standing quietly in the shadow), light from an opened door spilled over the flags.

A young redheaded woman passed through it, as a young redheaded man—clearly a brother or a cousin—came up beside her. They disappeared, displaced by others rushing to join the villagers gathering on the grass. But Mrowky had given Uk an elbow in the forearm; and, in the darkness, his breathing had increased to a tempo Uk knew meant the little man now had the grin which said, "I like that girl—she's hot!"

When the lights had rolled onto the common, Uk and Mrowky had moved up to the edge of the illuminated space, per orders. As, with his microphone, Nactor had ridden out to address the villagers, Uk wondered, as he did so often, just out of sight, whether the populace ever really saw them—or not. Just how aware were the stunned and disoriented peasants of the soldiers in their armor, waiting for the word?

In two years, Mrowky and Uk had been through this maneuver seventeen times in seventeen villages. It had taken the first half dozen for Uk to realize that it did not matter whether the villagers surrendered or not; the attack came in either case. Over those half dozen times, Uk had listened to Nactor's amplified address, watched the elimination of the spokesman (that's how it was referred to: though in a half a dozen villages now, the spokesman had been a woman), and awaited the final order with a growing distaste—till, by the seventh time, he'd begun to block out the whole thing.

Over the first ten times (which is how many times it had taken Mrowky to learn what Uk had learned in six), Mrowky had watched the process with hypnotic fascination, awed at its duplicity, its daring, its distractionary efficacy. But his attention span would have been strained by any more; so now he too gave no more mind to the details than did the other soldiers.

When the attack sounded you pulled out your sword, moved forward, and began to swing. You tried not to remember who or what you hit. A lot of blood spurted on your armor, and got in the cracks, so that you got sticky at knees and elbows and shoulders; otherwise it was pretty easy. The villagers were naked— most of them—and scared and not expecting it.

Among his first encounters, Uk, out of what he'd thought was humanitarianism, had—with some forethought—not always swung and cut to kill. It seemed fitting to give the pathetic creatures at least a chance to live. Three days later, though, he'd seen what happened to the ones who were just badly wounded: the long loud deaths, the maggoty gashes, the bone-breaking fevers, the cracked lips of the dying. . . . After that, from the same humanitarianism, he'd used his skills to become as deadly as he could with each blade swing at the screaming, clamoring folk—who simply had to be decimated.

That was orders.

Indeed, there was some skill to it—like avoiding the flesh-burning power beams lancing through the mayhem from the mounted officers. Best thing to do (Uk had explained to Mrowky a long time back, when the little guy'd gotten a burn on his right hip), was to glance up from the carnage now and then and keep Kire's horse a little before you, not drifting too far to the left or the right of it—since the mounted lieutenants had the sense (most of them) to avoid powergunning down each other.

You fought.

And you tried not to remember individual slashes and cuts you dealt out to bare shoulders and ribs and necks. (After the diseases and lingering deaths among the wounded in that first campaign, Uk tried for lots of necks.) Sometimes, though, an incident would tear itself free in the web of perception and refuse to sink back into the reds and blacks and chaotic grays and screams and crashes and howls that were the night.

When what happened next stopped happening—

But it was too violent and too painful for Rahm to recall with clarity.

He remembered walking backward, shouting, then—when Tenuk fell against him, like a bubbling roast left too long on the spit and so hot he burned Rahm's arms—screaming. He remembered his feet's uneasy purchase on the flags because of the blood that sluiced them. He remembered a dark-glazed crock smashing under a horse hoof. (With the soldiers, horror spread the village.) He remembered running to the town's edge, to find the gravefield shack aflame.

Ienbar had called, then shouted, then shrieked, trying to get past the fire from the mounted soldiers' muzzles; then Rahm hadn't been able to see Ienbar at all for the glowing smoke, and there'd been the smell of all sorts of things burning: dried thatch, wood, bedding, charred meat. Rahm had run forward, toward the fire, till the heat, which had already blinded him, made him—the way someone with a whip might make you—back away, turn away, run away, through the town, that, as his sight came back under his singed brows, with the chaos and the screams around him, was an infernal parody of his village.

* * *

Uk pulled his sword free to turn in the light from one of the towers, parked by an uncharacteristically solid building with a stone foundation. Something was wrong with Uk's knee; it had been throbbing on and off all last week; for three days now it had felt better, but then, only minutes ago, some soldier and some peasant, brawling on the ground in the dark, had rolled into him—Uk had cried out: it was paining him again. Turning to go toward the lit building, he'd raised his sword arm to wipe the sweat from under his helmet rim with his wrist—and smeared blood across his face, sticking his lashes together. But that had happened before. Grimacing at his own stupidity, he'd tried to blink the stuff away.

While he blinked, Uk recognized, between the struts of the light-tower, from the diminutive armor and a motion of his shoulder, Mrowky—who was holding somebody. Three steps further, knee still throbbing, Uk stopped and grinned. The little guy had actually got the redheaded girl—probably snagged her as she'd fled the common's carnage.

You're a lucky lady, Uk thought. Because Mrowky would do his thing with her, maybe punch her up a little, afterward, just to make her scared, then run her off. That was Mrowky's style—even though, when a whole village had nearly gone into a second revolt over the petitions, laments, and finally rebellious preachings of a woman raped by a soldier, Nactor himself had harangued the troops a dozen campaigns back: "I don't care *what* it is—boy, woman, or goat! You put a cock in it, you put your *sword* through it when you *finish* with it! That's an order—I don't *need* to deal with things like this!" But Mrowky wasn't comfortable—nor was Uk—killing someone just because you'd fucked her. And rarely did a woman carry on afterward like the one who'd raised Nactor to his wrath, especially if you scared her a little. Though others among the soldiers, Uk knew, honestly didn't care.

Really though, Uk thought, if Mrowky was going to do her now, he'd best take her out from under the light—behind the building; not for propriety, but just because Nactor or one of the officers might ride by. (No, Uk reflected, Mrowky wasn't too swift.) Favoring his right leg, Uk started forward to tell his friend to take it around the corner.

The redhead, Uk saw, over Mrowky's shoulder, had the stunned look of all the villagers. She was almost three inches taller than the little guy. Mrowky had one hand wrapped in her hair, so that her mouth was open. As his other hand passed over it, the redhead's arm gave a kind of twitch.

Which is when Uk heard the howl.

From the darkness, black hair whipping back and a body under it like an upright bull's, the big man rushed, naked and screaming. Rush and scream were so wild that, for a moment, Uk thought they had nothing to do with Mrowky and the girl; they would simply take this crazed creature through the light and into the dark again. Then Uk glimpsed the wild eyes, that, as the light lashed across them, seemed explosions in the man's head. The teeth were bared—the image, Uk thought later, of absolute, enraged, and blood-stopping evil. Under his armor, chills reticulated down Uk's shoulders, danced in the small of Uk's back.

The wild peasant was heading right toward Mrowky and the girl.

All Uk had a chance to do was bark Mrowky's name (tasting blood in his mouth as he did so); the careening man collided with them; for a moment he covered—seemed even to absorb—them both. Then he whirled. With a great sweep of one arm, he tore Mrowky's helmet from his head—which meant the leather strap must have cut violently into Mrowky's neck before it broke—if it didn't just tear over his chin and break Mrowky's nose. The big peasant whirled back; and Uk saw that he had Mrowky by the neck, in both of his hands—the guy's hands were huge, too! And Mrowky was such a little guy—

With sword up and aching knee, Uk lunged.

The big man bent back (a little taller than Uk, thicker in the chest, in the arms, in the thighs), drew up one bare foot and kicked straight out. The kick caught Uk in the belly. Though he didn't drop it, Uk's sword went flailing. He reeled away, tripped on something, and went down. Blinking and losing it all because of the blood in his eyes, Uk pushed himself up again; but the redhead was gone (doubtless into the dark he'd been about to urge Mrowky into) and the peasant, still howling, was flinging—yeah, flinging!—Mrowky from one side to the other, backing away. Mrowky's head—well, a head doesn't hang off *anyone's* neck that way! And the peasant was backing into the dark—was gone into it, dragging Mrowky with him!

Uk got out a curse, got to his feet, got started forward—and tripped on another villager who was actually moving. Wildly, he chopped his blade down to still her. (Yeah, in the neck!) Then he started off in the direction they'd gone, but not fast enough, he knew—damn the knee!

On the roof of Hara's hut, Qualt crouched, watching Rimgia, watching Rahm, watching Uk. (But he tried not to watch what Rahm was doing to the little soldier whose helmet Rahm had torn free.) Qualt turned away. Behind him something huge and dark and shadowy spread out from him on both sides, moving slightly in the breeze, like breathing—watching too. When he looked back, Qualt saw Rimgia stagger into the shadows around the councilhouse corner—and, in the shadows, saw Abrid run up to her, seize her by the shoulder, demand if she were all right, and, somehow, over the length of his own request, realize that she was not; and slip his other arm around her. Looking right and left, and totally unaware of what had gone on just around the corner (Rimgia's eyes were fixed and wide, as if she were seeing it all again), Abrid helped his sister off along the council-building wall.

Qualt had gripped the edging of twigs and thatch so tightly that even on his hard and callused palms it left stinging indentations. His hands loosened now, and he moved forward, as if to vault down and pursue them. But the thing

behind him—did it reach for his shoulder? No,
for it had not quite the hands we do. But a dark
wing swept around before him, like a shadow
come to life to restrain whoever would bolt
loose.

And turning, Qualt whispered, words lurching between heart beats that still near deaf-
ened, halting as the trip from one roof—over
the violence—to another: ". . . this is—what
thou seest if . . . thou flyest at Çiron!"

Something had happened to Rahm—not to the
part of him staggering through the chaos of villagers and soldiers. Rather, it happened to the
part growing inside—the thing that had begun
forming when the bearded rider had shot Kern.
It had needed a long time to grow: minute after
minute after minute of mayhem. But the growing thing finally got large enough to fill up and
join with something in Rahm's hands, in
Rahm's thighs, in Rahm's gut. It filled him, or
became him, or displaced him—however he
might have said it, they all referred to the
same. And when, from the darkness, Rahm
had seen Rimgia and the little soldier leaning
against the council building, saw him touch
her that way in the overhead light, the thing
inside, jerking and bloating to its full size, had
taken him over, muscle and mouth, foot and
finger.

When what happened next finished happening, Rahm had dragged the soldier halfway
through the town—till he no longer pulled at
Rahm's wrists, till he no longer flailed, struggled, gurgled, till he was limp and still and
hung from Rahm's grip, as Rahm stood in dark-

ness—choking out one and another rib-wrenching sob.

Horses' hooves struck around him. Rahm heard a shout beside him. A blade—Rahm saw firelight run up sharpened metal—cut at his shoulder; and a sound that was not a sob but a roar tore up out of him. He'd hurled the little soldier's corpse away (the flung body struck the sword from the soldier's hand, knocked the soldier free of his horse) and fled—till much later Rahm hurled his own body, nearly a corpse, down among the foothills.

He lay in the woods at the mountains' base, his cheek on his wrist; tears ran across the bridge of his nose, slippery over the back of his hand. Breath jerked into his lungs every half minute.

He lay in the leaves, gasping. His eyes boiled in their bone cauldrons. His teeth clenched so tightly, it was surprising the enamel of one or another molar did not crack. His body shook now and again, as if someone struck him hugely, on the head, on the foot. What kept going through his mind was, mostly, names. Names. In the dark woods, he tried to remember all the names he had spoken that day, from the time he'd first reached the field to the time he'd stood in the common. He would start to go through them, get lost—then try doggedly to start again, to remember them all this time. (What were they, again? What were they . . . ?) Because, he knew, a third of those names—children's, mothers', fathers', friends'—were no longer names of live people. And they mustn't be forgotten. But his body, finally, shook a little less. They must *not* . . . Without his mind ever really stilling—

—dawn struck Rahm awake with gold.

He rolled and stood in a motion, blinking to erase unbearable dreams. He stood a long time. Once he turned, looked down the wooded slope, then off into the trees either side. He began to shake. Then, possibly to stop the shaking, he started to walk—lurching, rather, for the first few minutes—upward. Possibly he walked because walking was most of what he'd been doing for the past week. And the relief from walking, the feeling of a wander at its end, the astonishing feeling of coming home—something terrible had happened to that feeling.

Rahm walked—

Once in a while, he would halt and shake his head, very fast—a kind of shudder. Then he walked again.

The trees thinned. As Rahm stumbled over the higher stones, bare rock lifted free of vegetation, to jut in crags around him—or to crumble under uncertain handholds. Soon he was climbing more than walking. After an hour—or was it two?—he came round a ledge, to find himself at a crevice. Fifteen feet high, a cave mouth opened narrowly before him.

CHAPTER
FOUR

From inside, a flapping sounded—as of a single wing.

Rahm eased along the ledge. Still numb, he had no sense of danger. His motivation was a less than passive curiosity—more the habitual actions of someone often curious in the past.

A fallen branch, split along its length, lay on the rock. Morning light reflected on the clean, inner wood, still damp from the breaking. Like metal. Like a polished sword gleaming in firelight—

Rahm grabbed up the stick, as if seizing the reality would halt the memory. He shook it—as if to shake free the image from it. Then, a moment on, the shaking turned to a hefting. One hand against the stone wall, the other holding the stick, Rahm stepped within the cave mouth, narrowing his eyes. A slant beam from a hole toward the roof lit something gray—something alive, something shifting, something near the rocky roof. That something moved, moved again, shook itself, and settled back.

Rahm stepped further inside. Looking up, frowning now, he called out—without a word.

A mew returned.

Rahm took another step. The gray thing made the flapping sound again.

As his eyes adjusted to the shadow, Rahm could make out its kite shape. It hung in a mass of filaments—one wing dangling. A tangle of webbing filled most of the cavity. Ducking under strands, Rahm took another step. Leaves ceased to crumble under his heel. Within, the softer soil was silent. He glanced when his foot struck something: a bone chuckled over rock. Rahm looked up again, raised his branch, brought its end near the trapped creature.

He didn't touch it. Between the branch's end and the leathery wing were at least six inches. But suddenly the mewing rose in pitch, turning into a screech.

Rahm whirled—because something had flung a shadow before him, passing through the light behind:

Suspended nearly four feet from the ground, a bulbous . . . *thing* swayed within the cave entrance, dropped another few inches—much too slowly to be falling—then settled to the ground. It scuttled across the rock, paused, made a scritting noise, then danced about on many too many thin legs. Rahm jabbed his stick toward it.

Mandibles clicked and missed.

It ran up the wall, then leapt forward. Rahm struck at it and felt the stick make contact. The thing landed, spitting, and hopped away, one leg injured and only just brushing the earth. Behind it trailed a gray cord—the thickness, Rahm found himself thinking, of the yarn Hara might use on her loom.

It jumped again. Rahm swung again.

Only it wasn't jumping at him; rather it moved now to one side of the cave, now to the other:

Two more cords strung across the cave's width.

And the cave was not wide.

Backing from it, Rahm felt his leg and buttock push against some of the filaments behind, which gave like softest silk. But as he moved forward again, they held to him—and when one pulled free of his shoulder, it stung, sharply and surprisingly.

This time, when it leaped across the cave, Rahm jumped high and, with his branch, caught it full on its body. It collapsed from the arc of its leap, landing on its back, legs pedaling. Rahm lunged forward, to thrust his stave through the crunching belly. Seven legs closed around the stick (the injured one still hung free): it scritted, it spat. Then all eight hairy stalks fell open. One lowered against Rahm's calf, quivered there, stilled, then quivered again. The hairs were bristly.

Blood trickled the stone, wormed between stone and dirt and, as all the legs jerked in a last convulsion—Rahm almost dropped his branch—gushed.

Rahm pulled the stick free of the carapace and stepped back, breathing hard. He looked up at the thing trapped in the webbing above. He looked down at the fallen beast on its back. And above again—where cords, leaves, sunlight, dust motes, and movement were all confused. He raised the stick among the filaments. He did not bring the end near the creature, but tried to pry among the threads in hope of breaking some—possibly even freeing it.

The branch went through them rather easily. The creature shifted above. Its free wing beat a moment.

Then, in a voice like a child's, but with an odd timbre under it not a child's at all, it said distinctly: "Use the blood!"

Rahm pulled his branch back sharply.

"To free me," the voice went on—strained, as though its position was manifestly uncomfortable, "use the blood!"

"Thou speakest . . . !" Rahm said, haltingly, wonderingly.

"Just like you, groundling! Big voice but stuck to the earth! Come on, I tell you . . . use the blood!"

Rahm stepped back again. Then, because his foot went lower down (on that slanted rock) then he expected it to, he looked back sharply so as not to trip.

The cave-beast's blood had rolled against one filament's mooring on the stone—the cord's base was steaming.

Now the filament came free, to swing over the cave floor. On a thought, Rahm pushed the stick's bloody end against a clutch of cords beside him. There was a little steam. Half the cords parted. When he felt something warm by his foot, Rahm looked down: blood puddled against his instep. But, though it parted the cords, against his flesh it didn't hurt or burn.

Rahm spoke, once more. "Thou wilt not hurt me if I free thee . . . ?"

"Free me and you are my friend!" The voice came on, like an exasperated child's. "Quickly now, groundling—"

"Because," Rahm went on, "I have been hurt too much when I thought what would come was friendship . . ."

What came from the trapped creature was the same sound that Rahm had already thought of as "mewing," though now, since the creature had spoken, the sound suddenly seemed to be articulated with all sorts of subtle feeling, meaning, and response, so that— had it been on a lower pitch—he might have called it a sigh.

Suddenly Rahm threw his stick aside, stepped back across the rock, reached down, and grabbed one of the dead thing's hairy legs, to drag it through the cave. By two legs, he hoisted it onto a higher rock shelf, climbed up beside it, then got it and himself to a shelf even higher. Squatting, he took a breath, frowned deeply—and wiped his hand across the gory wound. Then he grasped first one cord, and another, to feel them tingle within his sticky grip, dissolving.

After popping a dozen, one more and the bound creature fell a foot. The free wing beat.

That voice—like a child who has something wrong with its breathing—declared: "You take care!"

The creature mewed again.

Once more Rahm smeared up a handful of blood and began to work.

Later he tried to recall how he put all those aspects that told of an animal together with that childish voice that still, somehow, spoke of a man. As Rahm tugged cords away from the incredible back muscles, some of the soft hair stuck or pulled loose—and the muscles flinched. But the membrane-bearing limb those muscles moved—what he'd started to think of as an arm—was thicker than his own thigh and more than triple the length of his leg! It was all webbed beneath with leathery folds, folded down and caught between spines that were impossible distortions of fingers— fingers *longer* than arms! The teeth were small in that grimacing mouth. Once, in the midst of the pulling and parting, he saw them and the wedge-shaped face around them laugh at something he himself had missed. But it was still good to see laughter in that face that was not a face, because the nose was broad as three fingers of a big-handed man laid together; the sides of the head were all veined ear; and the eyes had pupils like a cat's—small as a cat's, too, which was strange, because, standing, at last, on the shelf of rock, with one long foot (whose big toe was as long as, and worked like, Rahm's thumb), the creature was a head shorter than Rahm. "Here, now—help me get my other foot free . . . ?" said this man, this beast, this Winged One with thigh and shoulder muscles as thick as little barrels.

Holding to rock, holding to that astonishing shoulder, Rahm leaned out, bloody handed, and caught another cord that dissolved in his grip. "Now—" he pulled back, with a quick grunt—"we must find some water to wash off this stinking stuff!" Small twigs and leaves caught up in the webbing fell to the cave floor.

"As a pup—" the Winged One grimaced, flexing—"I used to sneak off with the rough and rude girls who went to collect these threads for our ropes and hunting nets—till my aunt caught me and said it was not fitting for one of my station. Well, don't you know, an hour ago, hanging with the blood a-beat in my ears, I was thinking how ironic that I'd most likely end my life lashed up in the sticky stuff, once the beast, crouching just above the cave entrance there inside, grew hungry!"

They climbed down, Rahm at a loss for what so many of the words (like *rude, fitting, station,* and *ironic*) might mean. "When I was a child," Rahm said, supporting the creature above him, "the elders of my village always taught us to fear thy people—and to stay clear of thee, should one of thee ever alight near our fields!"

"As well you should!" declared the high voice, as the wings, all wrinkled and stretched not a full fifth of their spread, still went wall to wall in that high, narrow cave. "We always tell our little ones, whenever they come near you, to act as frightening as they can—before they fly away! Oh, my friend, we've heard—and seen!—some of the things your kind can do to its own. And that does not portend well for what you might do to our kind or others. Oh, I don't mean your own village in particular— Çiron at the mountain's foot. But we fly far of Hi-Vator, and we fly wide of Çiron; and we listen carefully—and often what we hear is not so good. So our elders have always thought a policy of self-containment, helped on by a bit of mild, if mutual, hostility, was best. I never took it seriously myself—though some I know do nothing else. Well, certainly, I'm glad it's broken through, here and now, in this direction.

"What's your name, groundling?"

"Rahm. And thine?"

The Winged One tilted his head. "Vortcir."

On the cave floor, Rahm bent, picked up the blood-blackened end of the branch he'd used to kill the cave-beast. He looked at it. Blood, dry now, had gone dark all over his fingers and palms and wrists, stuck about with dirt. "And how wert thou trapped by this thing, Vortcir?"

The Winged One cocked his head the other way. The short creature's great shoulders lifted their folded sails—half again as high as Rahm—and brought them in around himself. "I was careless." The expression (on that face that seemed to have so few of them) was embarrassment. "In the night, I fled into its cave, unaware that the danger I fumbled into was greater than the one I fled."

"What danger didst thou flee?"

Vortcir's face wrinkled. "In the night a great wailing came to deafen us. It filled us with fear and we scattered from our nests, blundering low among the trees, yowling higher than the crags, till, unable to find our way, I saw many of my people driven mad by that terrible wailing. I could hear the echo from this cave. I flew in here, thinking the sound would be less. But I flew into the web and, by struggling, only entangled myself more. And when I excited the cave-beast enough, it would come over and throw another couple of threads about me. *Uhh!*" Vortcir paused. "But you arrived . . . how is it that you stray so high among the mountains, groundling Rahm?"

Rahm waited while a wind stilled outside in the rocks. "I too fled the great wailing that came last night."

"I hear in your voice many strange things," said Vortcir, frowning. "Will you now go down to your nest?"

"My . . . nest has been destroyed."

"Destroyed? While I hung here, wound in that dreadful web, in this sound-deadening cave? Çiron? How is that?"

Rahm turned suddenly and flung the blackened branch against the cave wall. He pulled his shoulders in. It was as if the thing that had come loose inside him shook, lurching into the body's walls. Rahm felt air on his back. Something on his back was a touch, but it touched so much of him. He looked up.

Vortcir moved his wing away from Rahm's shoulder. The triangular face was puzzled. "You have saved my life," Vortcir said. "By this, we are friends. What, friend Rahm, is this thing that makes your heart roar and the muscles sing on your bones with anger?"

"Thou dost hear the sounds of my heart and bone?"

"And of your tongue's root, a-struggle in your throat for words, as if it would tear itself

free of your mouth. My people have keen . . ."
followed by a word that probably meant "hearing," for the great veined leaves of Vortcir's
ears flicked forward, then back.

Rahm looked out at the leaves beyond the
cave mouth. "Let us wash this blood from ourselves." His own voice was hoarse. "Is there a
stream?"

"You do not hear where the water is, right up
there . . . ?" Vortcir's wing tip bent down in
what first seemed a wholly awkward manner—
till Rahm realized he was pointing with it.

Rahm frowned.

"Let us go wash." Vortcir grinned. "And you
may tell me what it is that hurts you so
deeply."

They left the cave. Rahm moved over the
rocks with long strides. Vortcir traveled in
short-legged jumps, his wings fanning now
and again for balance.

"Vortcir," Rahm said, as they walked, "my
people go naked on the ground. Thy . . . people
go naked in the air. Both are easy with the land
about them. We fight with our hands and our
feet—and then only what attacks. We love our
own kind and are at peace with what lies about
us. But . . . this is not true of all creatures . . ."
In a low, quick voice, Rahm began to tell what
he had seen happen in the streets of his village
last night. As the tale went on, it finally
seemed, even to him, simply outrage strung
after outrage—so that at last he stopped.

Rahm looked at Vortcir. His amber eyes
seemed some substance once molten that had
recently set to a shocking hardness.

". . . But what fills me with terror, Vortcir, is

that the evil now is in me—too. I am filled with it. Yesterday morning, I killed a lion. This morning I killed the cave creature. And both of them were a kind of sport. But last night, Vortcir, I killed a man—a man like myself; a man as thou. I held his neck in my hands; and I squeezed, and I twisted it till . . ." As they reached the mountain stream, Rahm stopped. He squatted by the water, let one knee go forward into the mud. "I am not who I was, Vortcir." As he began to wash, around his arms water darkened; not all the blood was from the fight in the cave. "Who I have become frightens me. I think perhaps I can not, or I should not, go back to my village."

Vortcir stepped into the water and squatted in it. One wing unfolded, began to beat against the water and wave about on it. "Why so?"

Rahm turned his face from the spray and spatter of the Winged One's washing—and grinned. The grin was at the splashing, not the thought. Still, it felt good to grin again. Rahm said: "Because if I would go down again, Vortcir, I would do the same to the neck of every blade-wielding soldier, of every black-cloaked officer still in the village of Çiron!" Behind his hard, hard eyes, Rahm was wondering what it meant to say what he said as seriously as he said it and still to grin as he was grinning.

But it felt good—even as it gave him chills.

Vortcir brushed drops from his face with his shoulder. "I hear you well, Rahm. Your people are good folk—we even watch you, time to time." Vortcir gave a quick laugh. "Perhaps yours are a finer people than my own. We strive for peace. But sometimes we do not achieve it.

We Winged Ones, as you call us—sometimes we kill each other. We know this is wrong. When one of our number kills another, we catch him and mete out punishment." He shrugged, an immense, sailed shrug. "It does not happen often." Vortcir turned and splashed about with his other wing.

Rahm picked up a handful of wet sand and used it to scrub at his arm, at his shoulder. When blood came away from the cut he'd received last night, it stung. He looked at squat Vortcir—who stood, feet wide in the rushing foam. Both wings opened now, Vortcir raised his head. He began to mew.

Rahm looked up.

Suddenly and excitedly, Vortcir called: "My aunt nears!" Then, at once, he leapt. Twigs and water drops flew about. Rahm closed his eyes against the rush of leaves and dirt.

When he opened them, Vortcir was clearing the broken cliff, rising before billowing cloud.

For a moment Rahm lost him. Then, a moment later, he saw two Winged Ones, moving together and apart, circling, meeting, one soaring away, the other soaring after—till, suddenly, both were alighting on the rocks at the stream's far bank.

Vortcir splashed forward, then turned and spoke somewhat breathlessly to the other: "Here is the groundling called Rahm who saved my life!"

The woman Winged One was a breadth larger than Vortcir in every direction: taller, deeper chested, broader sailed. She wore a brass chain around her neck—and was clearly the elder. "You are a friend, then, groundling?"

While rougher and aged, her voice was as high and as breathy as her nephew's. "You have saved my fine boy; all men and women who fly will be grateful to you and give you honor."

The grin had gone. There was only a smile on Rahm's face now: "All . . . ?"

"Vortcir is Handsman of our nest!" she declared as if that explained everything. "Will you now come with us?"

Smiling mirth became smiling wonder: "Where—?"

"To our nest in the high rocks—to Hi-Vator!"

"But how could I climb after thee, if—"

"Easily!" Mewing, Vortcir turned to his aunt. "He's tall—but scrawny! He can't weigh much. Come, friend Rahm! Climb on my back."

"Canst thou support me?" Rahm stood at the water's edge. He had never thought of himself as light. But, shorter than Rahm by a head, still Vortcir was half again as heavy.

Rahm stepped across the water and behind Vortcir, who turned and bent to take him. Rahm grasped him over the shoulders. The furred back bunched beneath Rahm's chest. On either side of him the leather sails spread, and spread, and spread! They did not beat—but vibrated, at first. Without any sense of motion at all—at first—the ground sank away. Then, at once, leaves in the trees above dropped toward them, fell below them. Rahm caught his breath—tightened his grasp. And the wings gathered and beat once more—and, yes, they flew!

Looking down over Vortcir's shoulder, Rahm saw far more rock below than green.

"How does it feel to fly, friend Rahm?" Vortcir called back; then he cried to his aunt: "He's light as a fledgling!" Vortcir's mew rose. Rahm peered over Vortcir's shoulder.

Some bare, some gorse-covered, rocks moved far below them. Wind stroked Rahm's arms, his buttocks, his back. The smell of the fur on Vortcir's neck was like the smell which might come from a casket or cabinet in Ien-bar's cabin, long locked and suddenly opened. Sometimes they flew so that Rahm hung against the thick back only by the hook of his arm. More often, they moved horizontally, so that Rahm lay prone on that body, broader than his own, even as his feet stuck free into the air. Sometimes it seemed they just floated, so that the sun warmed Rahm's neck and the trough between his shoulders, and no wind touched him at all. At others, the wind pum-meled Rahm's face and his arms and chilled his fingers (locked against Vortcir's chest), till he wondered if he could hold much longer. The excitement of flight contracted Rahm's stom-ach and, sometimes, made his heart hammer. He hugged more tightly to the flexing back.

Others had joined Vortcir and his aunt. As they descended, pitted cliffs rose. At last Vort-cir's feet scraped rock. Rahm caught his bal-ance and stood alone once more, arms and chest tingling, while he looked at the great, windy back-beating maneuvers of the others landing about them—or at Vortcir's own wing-beating, that finally stilled.

Drawing in his sails and breathing quickly (but not deeply; deep breaths seemed reserved for flight itself), Vortcir turned. "At Hi-Vator, here on the world's roof, now you will see how those who fly can live."

Others crowded in, then. There was a general cry: "Vortcir! Handsman Vortcir! Vortcir has returned!"

Vortcir's aunt pushed through. "But young Handsman—where is your chain of trust?"

Again Rahm noticed the chain around her own neck.

"I must have lost it when we were set upon by the terrible wailing."

"You cannot very well go without it. As I wear the sign and trust of a Queen, so must our Handsman wear the sign and trust of one ready at any moment to become King."

While this was going on, Rahm looked and blinked and looked again at these furred people, who stood so close to one another—in threes, fives, or sevens, always touching—but who, now and then, would explode into the air, soaring fifty, seventy-five, a hundred-fifty yards away from any fellows.

Already, in the margins of his take-off with Vortcir and his aunt, at the rim of their ride together, and at the edge of their landing with the others, Rahm had learned that these were a people among whom the women's furry breasts were scarcely larger than the men's, and that the men's genitals were almost as internal as the women's. The distinction between the sexes was only minimally evident, till one paused to urinate, as that male over there was doing, or when one of them was (as he realized at a glance to his left, where several were joking about a young female who evidently was) in a state of sexual excitement.

Carefully, while trying not to be caught staring, Rahm watched them. And, in their close, nervous groups, with their small eyes they watched him back. They watched him from ledges above. They watched him from the rope nets strung from staid oak branch to staunch hemlock trunk—apparently the youngsters' favorite place to play. They watched him from other, broader nets, strung from the rocks down by the water to the higher ledges, thirty and forty yards overhead—where, it seemed, the elderly gathered to gossip, stretching their wings till they quivered. The watching was particularly strange because, by now Rahm knew, they were doing more listening than looking. What, he wondered, could they hear of him, through their constant, mewing intercourse.

Within his first thirty minutes at Hi-Vator, Rahm saw a group of six winged children tease a smaller and younger child unmercifully. The older ones were—as far as he could tell—all boys. The little one was—most probably—a girl. The teasing reached such intensity that, twice, it became violent: had he been in his own home, Rahm would have stepped in to stop it. But now he could only look about uncomfortably for Vortcir or his aunt, both of whom happened, for the moment, to be somewhere else. Why, he wondered wildly, weren't any other adults paying attention . . . ?

Within his first three hours there, Rahm observed a game where you sailed cunningly constructed toys made of twigs and thin leather from ledge to ledge, then took them into the sky to sail them from flyer to flyer. Also he saw two other children playing with a lemur-like pet. Then he became involved in what he only realized was another game after fifteen minutes of it, as first one then another Winged One politely volunteered to fly him now to this ledge, now to another, now to still one more: and he would grasp the warm, heavy shoulders and be carried here and there around the many ledges of the gorge in which their cave dwellings were sunk, each side of a silvery feather of falling water. Rahm had already noted, upon landing, that it was a lot easier to tell the sex of the Winged One—strong young female or male—who'd just carried him. From the giggling together of those waiting to ferry him about, or others who had just finished, Rahm realized—with sudden humor—that, somehow, with them, this flying and carrying was a sexual game: and some others, he saw now, didn't approve!

For ten minutes later three older ones marched up and put a rather gruff end to it. The ones who'd been playing with him fluttered off. The older ones apologized to him in a way that, though he smiled and nodded and shrugged a lot, he didn't quite see the point of—since there was no harm in it.

Three hours more, and he'd discovered that while the Winged Ones' word for "star" was the same as his, they had no single word for "ear," but more than ten for its various parts and functions—also, from repeated inquiry, he finally decided they had no concept at all of the "tomato plant."

"What are you thinking, my friend?" Vortcir asked, suddenly at his side, when Rahm, in those first three hours, had once more gone still a moment, to stare off at those furry youngsters wrestling together by the falling water's edge, or at the creatures who seemed to be grinding some sort of grain in the great circular stone troughs behind them, or just at the clouds behind them all, in the luminous mid-morning sky.

"I am thinking," Rahm said, slowly and with consideration, "that, with perhaps here and there an exception that perplexes me—" he was recalling the children's particularly violent teasing—"thou art a people, a people very like my own."

And sitting in the sunlight, cross-legged on the blanket beside the wheel of his garbage cart, Qualt broke open a papaya. As its black seeds in their rich juice spilled out over the orange flesh in the morning sun, Qualt said: "Then, from what thou tellest me—with perhaps here and there something I do not quite understand—thy folk at Hi-Vator are . . . a people too; a people much like mine." And the similarity of what Qualt said to what—miles up the mountain—Rahm was saying (and the vastly differing situations in which each said it) should begin to speak to you of the true differences between Qualt and Rahm.

Qualt tossed half the fruit.

Perched on the wooden frame of some overturned bench that was not used any more in the village, but which sat here among the detritus lying about in the young garbage collector's yard, it reached out a great wing. The tines at its end caught the fruit and brought it back to the small, dark face. It bit, and juice and seeds ran down the fur at both sides of the mouth. It mewed, resettling itself. "Good! Hey, groundling—my sister was a rude, rough girl who went with the other poor girls to collect the filaments the cave-beasts spin, up in the rocks, to make our ropes and hunting nets and webs. But I was only a mischief maker, too lazy even to help them there. No, my people often thought that I was not a good one. So I took to wandering—flying here, flying there, listening now to these ones, now to those! Even when I was coming back, I saw one of your men, fighting with a lion, and dropped to give him my help, but one of those others seared my wing with the kind of flaming evil we saw last night—"

"It's a killing evil!" Qualt bit his fruit. "And that's why thou must do as I say. If we keep on, my friend, like we've begun this morning—"

At which point there was ringing from behind the house.

Qualt was on his feet. "Quick now, as I told thee—" He sprinted off between the junk strewn about the yard toward the house corner, to step around it, over moist rocks and three piles of old pots, some broken, some nested in one another, hollyhocks grown up between them.

The path up to the garbage collector's shack was narrow, and you couldn't walk without brushing the low branches. Long ago Qualt had strung a rope between those branches which, if any of them were hit, rang a goat's bell he'd fixed to a post near the front door.

"Hey, there, Qualt," came a familiar voice.

Old Hara pushed from the path end. "I wondered if you were home, there . . ."

Qualt went forward.

"Ah, boy, this is a deadly day!" Yes, it was Hara, with the white in her hair like the froth of the quarry falls, with her skirt the colors of leaves and earth and hides. "Phew!" Her face wrinkled even more, as she came barefoot toward the house. "How do you stand the stink?"

"Why dost thou come here, Hara? Why dost thou come here after what happened in the town last night?"

The weaver shook her head. "I go to a council-meeting. You know that Ienbar, among so many, was killed—burned to death at his shack by the burial meadow."

"Not Ienbar, too? But where are they meeting, Hara? Not in the council building?"

The old woman shook her head. "No, boy— the Myetrans are there now. But it's not a meeting you can linger about the edges and overhear. Not this time." She reached out and pushed the side of Qualt's head playfully with her knuckles. "Oh, maybe when a bit more of youth's foolishness has gone out of thee and some more of wisdom has settled between thy ears—but there's no need for anyone to know where we meet now. The Myetrans are still about all over the town. And they do not want us meeting. No, not after last night—"

"Yes," Qualt said. "I see—" Hara crossed toward the corner of the house. Qualt hurried after her, just as she stepped around the pots and hollyhocks. But the back yard, with the varied junk strewn about in it, and the garbage cart to the side, was empty.

"It won't be an easy meeting, though—I tell you, boy! There's seven hundred and forty people here at Çiron—oldsters and babes among us. While the Myetrans—well, there are thousands of them, it seems! And we have to figure out a way to—"

"Hara," Qualt said. "Hara, there're *not* thousands of them!"

She stopped and looked at him.

Qualt crumpled the papaya rind and flung it into the bushes. "There're not thousands of them. There're not hundreds of them! There're a hundred-eighty-seven. Perhaps I'm off by five or six—up or down. But not by more!"

Hara frowned. "And how dost thou know, little dirty-fingers?"

"Because I counted!"

"When didst thou count?"

"Earlier this morning. They get their camp up at sunrise—and I . . . I counted. A hundred-eighty-seven. A few more than half of them are in the village. Somewhat less than half are at their camp. There's a group of five, whom all the others obey. They stay in three tents that are larger than the others, at the back of the encampment—the mounted one with the beard who killed Rimgia's father last night is one of them. Then, among the rest, there are ten who wear the black clothes, with the black cloaks and hoods—who ride horses and tell their men, the ones who have only the swords and their metal and leather plates bound to them, where to go and what to do. The black ones and the five leaders alone have the power-guns—the things they killed Kern and Tenuk and . . . killed so many with. Powerguns are what they call them—someone overheard them speak the word, and told me. And there're no more than twenty powerguns among them—and a dozen are resting, at any one time. That's another thing they have to do—after they fire them twenty or thirty times they have to let them rest a while, so they'll regain their fire. Someone—I heard them joking about them when they rounded up some forty-three of our people, wounded all, but who could still walk, and herded them into a wire corral where they have them imprisoned—"

"Forty-three of us imprisoned?" Hara exclaimed. "Ah, thank the generous earth! For in town, they've started to count the bodies of those who were killed—and there seemed to be more than thirty missing. Do you know who the corralled ones are, Qualt? Do you know which ones are their prisoners? You tell us that, and it would ease a lot of sick hearts, boy—"

"I can tell you that: and I can tell you more—though I'll have to learn it later. But there are ten in black, who, with the five leaders, have the powerguns."

Hara had started walking again.

"But tell the council, Hara! There are five in charge. And only a hundred-eighty-seven all together—give or take four or five . . . !"

"You can believe I'll tell them, boy! You can believe it—" Hara went on toward the quarry road, making for wherever the village council had decided to hold its meeting.

Qualt stood in the yard, breathing hard—as though the imparting of the information had been a sudden and painful effort.

You see, he was a very different person from Rahm.

Over the edge of Qualt's roof thrust a sharp face with scooped ears. A moment later, a shadow flapped—

Qualt turned as the Winged One moved out onto the air—as if air were water and the Winged One pushed off into it as Qualt might push off from the quarry shore . . . and Qualt himself were looking up at it as a fish might look from the lake bottom.

The Winged One sailed over the yard—full of the things that, now and again, curious Qualt had rescued from the irredeemable arc into the ravine, a kind of sculpture garden of furniture, farm equipment, and even more unrecognizable stuffs, pieces leaning in odd positions, an occasional rope from one to the other from which some pot or bit of houseware hung.

Flapping wings settled, till the Winged One perched on the corner of Qualt's garbage wagon. One sail out for balance, the Winged One moved the other's edge across his mouth, knocking away the little seeds that had stuck to his face fur. "Say, groundling—there! You've told what we learned aloft this morning to one of your elders, like you wanted. Do you think that now you'll let me take you up to Hi-Vator? There it would be fun—and you wouldn't have to hide like you say I have to here . . . ! Though there I might still have to hide from a few, because some folk there—some even of my own family—do not like me as much as all that!"

The Winged One laughed out shrilly, the mighty sails out full—on which, with the sunlight behind them, Qualt could see scars that spoke of violence and adventure. "Sometimes I think I can not—or perhaps I should not—go back to Hi-Vator. Oh, there're not many up there who listen for my return. Other times I think maybe I should go visit them, with one of you groundlings on my back to surprise them, as though I were a Handsman or a noble, who could make and break such laws at will. But if I could make and break such laws, then I would not be the outlaw I am. Oh, I assure you—I'm only a little outlaw. Don't fear me, friend. I never broke any *big* laws. I just forget and do what I want sometimes, and discover it wasn't what someone else wanted me to do. Then I have to fly . . ."

"Yes," Qualt said, absently. "This law, that thou spokest of earlier. Now what is this 'law' that you are outside of, as thou sayest—"

But the Winged One just laughed. "I know, groundling! Perhaps we can roll around together on the earth the way we did last night—that was fun too, 'ey? Or would you like to try it in the air? That was a good game, no?—even if it only came by the accident of that awful sound, so that I could not tell where I was when I flew into you! You groundlings do it in the dirt. We Winged Ones do it in the—"

But suddenly Qualt turned, vaulted up on the bench of the garbage cart, and stood erect on the seat while the wheels creaked below them both. "No, my friend—there'll be a later time for Hi-Vator." Qualt stepped behind the creature's great sail, like an object rejoining a shadow that had been momentarily lost to it by a mystery beyond naming. "Yes, like last night, we'll fly a bit more at Çiron!"

By his final three hours at Hi-Vator, Rahm had decided that, no, the Winged Ones were a very, *very* different people from his—but that it was precisely those differences that *made* them a people. With each new thought or realization or insight about them, however, there came a moment when Rahm would stand, now for seconds, now for minutes, still as the cliffs rising above him, his mind fallen miles below, turning among memories of the light- and blood-lashed night, trying to hold coherent the idea of a people of his own. When he stood so long like that, some of the Winged Ones watched or listened quietly. Others, better mannered, merely listened and pretended not to watch at all—though more and more mewed about it to one another, out of sight and hearing.

Among the stranger things that had happened to him that afternoon was a conversation he'd had with an old Winged One, whom Vortcir had been eager to have him meet for more than an hour now. The Winged One's fur was more gray than brown. Her eyes were wrinkled closed.

Rahm and the ancient creature hung together on one of the rope webs, above the waterfall, while the old Winged One explained to Rahm that one of the most important ideas around which all the Winged Ones' lives revolved was something called god—apparently a very hard thing to understand, since it was at once the universal love binding all living things and, at the same time, a force that punished evil-doers even as it forgave them: also it was a tree that grew on the bare peak of the world's highest mountain, a tree older than the world itself, a tree whose roots required neither earth nor water—those roots having secreted the whole of the world under it, including the mountain it perched on. The tree's leaves were of gold and iron. Its fruit conferred invisibility, immortality, and perfect peace. To make things even more complicated, for just a short while—twenty-nine years to be exact, the old Winged One explained—god had not been a tree at all, but rather a quiet, good, and simple woman with one deformed wing, who therefore could not fly and thus limped about the mountains' rocks like a groundling. Various and sundry evil Winged Ones would come across her and try to cheat her, or to rob her, or—several times—even attempt to kill her, only to be shamed by a power she had, called "holiness," whereupon they repented and—often—became extremely good, fine, and holy people themselves for the rest of their lives, during which they did nothing but help other Winged Ones.

"There are other peoples," the old Winged One told Rahm, as she stretched over the knotted vines, "who represent god as a silver crow, while for others god is a young man strung up to die on a blasted tree . . ." which only confused Rahm further.

Still, something about the old Winged One made her comforting to listen to. Something in her manner recalled . . . Ienbar? The stories of the flightless god were gentle and good and took Rahm's mind off the cataclysmic images that lazed just under memory's surface.

Rahm climbed down from the rope net, curious as to why he felt better, but not convinced that this idea/tree/cripple was much more than a story with too many impossibilities to believe, so that while it might have had something he couldn't quite catch to do with the world around him now, he couldn't believe it had much to say of the world he'd left below.

The afternoon sun had lowered enough to gild the western edge of every crag and rock. At the fire Winged Ones adjusted three mountain goats on wooden roasting spits. Walking up to another ledge, Rahm saw some others pounding nuts on a large rock with small stones held in their prehensile toes. Still others, on the ledge above that, had gathered hip-high heaps of fruit—yellow, purple, and orange—so that when, a few minutes later, Vortcir's aunt came up to him and said: "There's to be a feast tonight!" Rahm was not really surprised.

"In honor of the Handsman's safe return?" Rahm asked.

"In honor of the groundling who saved him!" she declared, shrill and breathy. Then, with wings wide, she turned to drop over the rocky rim at his feet and crawl down a web.

Winged Ones carried a trestle over, piled with fruit and nutbread. "Have some," Vortcir urged him. "Some of us have flown leagues and leagues to bring these to the nest." They brought a chain for Vortcir—who insisted they bring another for Rahm. Vortcir's aunt herself held it on the spurs of her wings and lowered it around Rahm's neck with cooling, windy motions. Several Winged Ones made music on a rack of gongs, while youngsters flapped and scrambled over the rocks, flinging the scarlet, cerise, and leaf-green rinds at each other, now at a furry arm, now at a leg jerked back, from which the peel peeled limply away, falling to the stone as the thrower mewed and the target squealed. Caves pitting the cliff-side site echoed with chucklings and chitterings. Across the twelve-foot fire troughs, the spitted carcasses rolled above flame, fat dribbling and bubbling along the bottom of each beast.

"Here, Rahm!" Vortcir led him up to a stone rim. "You must make the first cut." On his spur, Vortcir lifted a great cleaver, long as his thigh. Rahm turned to seize it by a handle carved for a grip wholly different from his own. He planted one foot on the pit-stone. Their wings beating up spirals of sparks, the fire tenders swung the first spit out. Rahm raised the blade—

His eyes caught the red light running up the sharpened metal—and, as he had done so many times that day, Rahm halted. His chest rose; breath stalled in it.

Some of the Winged Ones fell silent.

One of Vortcir's wings opened to brush and brush at Rahm's back, to smear the sweat that had, in moments, risen on Rahm's shoulders, his forehead, his belly. "Friend Rahm, this blade is to cut the meat that we will all eat. Use it!"

Rahm swung the cleaver down. Crusted skin split. Juices rilled and bubbled along the metal. And Rahm grinned. The others chittered and laughed and mewed. Some even came up to compliment him on the dexterity with which he carved: "But then, you have so many little fingers. . . ."

Lashed to a wooden fork, a leather sack dripped wine into a stone tub, from which, at one time or another, everyone went to drink. Three times Rahm found himself at the rim beside a female with granite-dark fur, a quick smile, and a sharp way of putting things in an otherwise genial manner. "So," she said, when the wine had made Rahm feel better and they met again a ways from the food, "I overheard you talking to that blind old fool about god," though she spoke the word "fool" with such affection as to make Rahm wonder if it meant the same to her as it did to him. "You know what the real center of our life here is? It isn't god."

"What is it, then?" Rahm asked.

Behind her, her wings . . . breathed, in and out of the indigo, out and into the firelight. "Actually, it's money."

"Money?" he asked. "Money . . . now, what is money?"

Apparently it was more complicated than god. It, too, she explained, was fundamentally an idea, having to do with value—in this case, represented by the hard hulls of certain nuts, treated with certain dyes, with certain symbols carved into them. You gave some of these hulls for everything you received, or got some back for everything you gave—Rahm was not sure which; "everything" included food, sex, and entertainment, labor, shelter, and having certain rituals performed for you by the Handsman or the Queen.

"I'd like to see some," he said, with polite interest, "of this money."

She cackled, in a scrit as shrill as that of the beast he'd slain in the cave. "But that's the whole problem, you understand. Nobody has any, anymore!"

He was confused all over.

"We gave it up," she explained, "years ago. When I was a girl—maybe eight or nine. We had a meeting of the whole nest site, and the Old Queen decided we'd be better off without it. So we went back to barter. But no one's really forgotten it—I don't care what the Old One says. Personally, I think it would be better if we had it back again, don't you?"

Around him the Winged Ones caroused through the deepening evening. Now and again, Rahm watched five, six, seven or more rise from jagged rocks, gone black against the blue, in what, for the first moments, was a single fluttering mass, to shrink in the distance and flake, finally, apart as single flyers. There, among them, was the young woman who'd just been talking to him about this money—how did he recognize her, in silhouette like that? (Had she taken part in the afternoon's forbidden game? Of that, he couldn't be sure.) But he did: definitely it was she, among the others, flying away.

With their mysterious and mystic notions—money and god—these folk had again begun to seem wholly foreign. Rahm raised his hand to finger the chain at his neck, that made him, at least honorarily, some sort of personage among these incomprehensible creatures. What, he wondered, would he tell one of the

Winged Ones who wanted to know what ideas were most central to his own, ground-bound nest site?

Behind him, Vortcir whispered, intensely: "Fly with me, friend Rahm!"

Rahm turned and, with an avidity that surprised him, threw his arms around that powerful neck, as Vortcir turned (in turn) to take him. Rahm bent one arm down across the flexing shoulder. "Watch that thou dost not crash the two of us onto the rocks!" Was Vortcir's head as full of wine as his . . . ?

The feeling, that he had almost grown used to by now, was that the Winged One who carried him took a great breath that finally just lifted his feet from the ground, a breath that didn't stop—the air itself taking them higher, and higher, and higher.

"This is a fine night to fly!" Vortcir called back.

Fires flickered below them. A file of Winged Ones flew just above the flame. Wing after wing reddened, darkened. Loosed from it all and looking down on it over the Handsman's shoulder, Rahm felt the whole nest site and all the flying folk he'd met there, children, adults, and oldsters, to be wondrously and intricately organized—as fine, as rich, and as logical as any folk could be.

"You like the life we lead, don't you?" came the child-voice.

Rahm nodded, his cheek moving against the Handsman's flour-scoop of an ear—which twitched against him.

"They are good men and women," Rahm said. They arched away from the cliff-side and the water's rush and the jutting trees, all black below them now. "They have all been kind to me."

"And you are happy," Vortcir said. "I can hear it."

Rahm said: "The wine has dulled thy hearing."

"For a moment—for several moments—" Vortcir shook his head in a kind of shiver, though his wings still pumped them steadily across the night—"you were happy. Will you stay with us, friend Rahm?" The only sound was the air, loud in Rahm's ears—though surely much louder in Vortcir's. "I have heard your answer." Beside them, the mountain rose.

Rahm spoke rather to himself than to Vortcir, because he already knew it was not necessary: "I want to go home . . ."

"I have heard," Vortcir repeated.

They descended the night.

"Where are we?" Rahm moved his feet in soil that held small rocks, leaves, and twigs. Neither moon nor stars broke the darkness.

"At the edge of the meadow where you bury your dead." Wide wings beat, not to fly but to enfold him, shaking on him and about him in a manner both affectionate and distressed. "Do not stumble—" the little voice sounded rough and close, as the wings parted—"on the corpses."

"Are there many about?"

"They have brought many. No one has buried them, yet. Friend Rahm . . . ?"

"Yes, Vortcir?"

"I must go back up now to my own people. But I will listen for you always." The high, breathy chuckle. "That's what we say when we leave a friend."

Rahm put his arms around Vortcir's shoulders once more, to grasp the creature to him who, in the dark, was only furred muscle, a high voice, a knee against his, a hot breath against his face and a scent more animal than human. Rahm stepped back. "And I will watch and . . . listen for thee! Vortcir . . . ?" Wind struck against him for answer. A little dust blew against his cheeks and got into one eye, making Rahm turn away, rubbing at it with his foreknuckle, so that the beating was at his back. Then it was above, thundering dully. Somewhere, as the sound stilled, a breeze rose over it with its own thunder of leaves and shushing grasses. (It brought with it an unpleasant smell, like rotting vegetables and clogged waters; but Rahm tried not to name it, or even pay attention to it.) When it stilled, all sound was gone.

Beneath Rahm's feet, grass gave way to path dust. He walked. Firelight flickered from inside a window. By one shack, he stopped to look in—through a crack between two logs under the sill; a crack, he realized, he'd peeped through many, many nights one winter, years ago, when someone else entirely had lived there.

A woman sat at the table, her head down, her shoulders hunched high. Two grown sisters had lived in this hut for the past half-dozen years. Rahm pulled away sharply when it struck him what it likely meant that only one was there tonight.

He turned and hurried across the road and ducked into the darkness between two houses. For a moment he wondered if he was lost, but, at the glow from another hut's shutter, open perhaps three inches, he realized where he was.

Going up to the dim strip of light, he looked through. On a table a lot more rickety than the one in the last hut, a clay lamp burned with a flame more orange than yellow. Sitting on a bench, back against the wall and staring straight forward, was a man—whose name Rahm didn't know.

But he knew those shoulders—and the short, spiky hair: and the face. The man, not half a dozen years older than Rahm, worked on one of the quarry crews, sometimes with Abrid and . . . Kern.

Odd, Rahm thought, that there are people in my town whom I really don't know—though I've seen them, now and again, all my life. I probably know the names and the names of most of the relatives of practically every field worker. But do I know more than a dozen of those who work in the stone pits . . . ?

The surprise, of course, was that the man lived *here*. But then, Rahm went on thinking, that is what makes this town mine. It still holds for me perfectly simple things to learn, like what the name is or where the house lies of one of its stone workers. . . .

Then the thought interrupted itself: Is he blind . . . ? The man's eyes were open. He looked right at the window. Only inches out in the darkness, Rahm could not believe himself unseen. But the man's expression was the complete blank of one who slept with his eyes wide. Standing in the darkness, concentrating to read that blankness, Rahm was equally still, equally blank—

The man started forward.

Rahm started back—but something held him.

The man was up, moving to the window. He looked out at Rahm, and gave a grunt—the way quarrymen so often did. "I thank thee," he said, softly, roughly—though Rahm had no idea why—and smiled. "But thou hast better go. The patrol comes soon." He pulled the window closed.

Rahm stood in the dark, bewildered by the exchange. What, he found himself wondering, would I have seen had I looked into this same window last night before the wailing? Two other quarry workers sharing the hut with him? Perhaps a woman—perhaps two?

Some children? What absences in the house today did the blankness—or the smile—mean?

The return from his wander the previous day had started Rahm pondering all he knew of his village. But his return tonight, after the violence of the night before and the wonders of the day, had started him pondering all he did *not* know of it.

Rahm crossed the dark path. Nearing the common, he walked by more close-set huts.

Old Hara the Weaver's cottage had never had a shutter—at least not on its back window. But a hanging had been tacked up across it—although, at one edge, it had fallen away so that a little light came through. Within, he could hear the old woman talking—to herself, Rahm realized, as, with his fingertips on the window ledge, he put his eye to the opening between the window edge and the cloth.

"They shall not have it! They shall not! I said it in the council, and I say it now: they shall not have it!" He could see Hara moving about before the fire, a sharp-shouldered figure. Now she put down an armful of cloth—and, taking up a cooking blade, she began to slash at one piece and another as she lifted them. "Never for them—they shall not!" With a hard, hard motion, she flung one handful and another of rags into the flames.

Rahm pulled back—even though the pieces did not flare.

He turned from the hut's sagging wall, to start away, when, from around the corner—

—lights, horses, hooves!

"There, Çironian! What are you doing out?"

Rahm whirled, hands up over his eyes against the light.

"You know the ordinance, Çironian. No windows or doors are to be open after dark! No man, woman, or child is to be on the street! You're under arrest! Come with us."

"With you—?" Rahm began, squinting between his fingers as he pulled them from his eyes.

"Anyone the patrol catches out past sundown is under arrest, Çironian. Do not make further trouble for yourself."

A rope dropped over his shoulders to be

yanked tight. Another soldier was down off his horse to grasp Rahm's hands and pull them behind him. "We'll take him with us on the rest of the patrol around the common, before we deliver him to the holding cell." Another rope went round his wrists.

As the horse in front started away, Rahm was tugged forward, so that he stumbled, nearly falling.

He kept his feet though. The feeling was a kind of numbness. (The other Myetran soldier was back on his horse now. Horses clopped on the street at both sides of him.) But within the numbness there was something else: it was a feeling hard for Rahm to describe. It was as if the thing that had, the night before, grown to fill him, that had almost become him, had now, at the horse's first tug, torn loose from him. It was as if his flesh had parted and the thing that had filled him had remained standing, unmoving on the street—so that only the rind of him was dragged away, a limp thing collapsing through the light-lashed dark.

Not that the thing left behind stayed still.

It followed. It came steadily, easily after them, even as Rahm stumbled on. It moved firmly, watched impassively. (For moments Rahm was convinced that if he glanced back, he would see it, coming after them, lowering in the dark.) It observed them, impartial, now like something circling them, now like something walking with them. That impartiality, that impassivity, that sheer chill, was more unsettling than the indifference of the soldiers in front of him and beside him, taking him through the streets about the common—because Rahm's stumbling was, anyway—most of it—feigned. When his wrists had yanked from the soldier's hands, the knot hadn't been pulled tight yet: it would have been nothing to bunch his fingers and, though the hemp might burn, wrench a hand free. The rope around his arms and chest was only, he was sure, one great shrug away from coming loose. These Myetrans, Rahm thought, were used to dealing with terrified men and women.

But, Rahm realized, as he stumbled and blinked in their passing lights, trying to look terrified and cringing, the thing that went with them—the thing that was really he—was *not* frightened. (Did they, Rahm wondered, find the sight of a frightened man or woman somehow beautiful? But they did not even look at him. Were they, perhaps, like the Winged Ones, listening? He did not think so.) It was not frightened at all.

CHAPTER
FIVE

From the corner of Hara's hut, Naä watched the soldiers ride off with Rahm. She had seen him at the first house, followed him to the second—recognizing him only in the light from the open shutter, before it closed (till now, she'd assumed him killed in the first night's massacre)—and come behind him quietly at the third. She'd followed him, through the breezy night, excitement growing, anticipating what he might say to her, his surprise at seeing her, his pleasure at knowing she was alive and free as he was, when finally she would overtake him with a word—

Really, she'd been *about* to speak—when the patrol had come up, and, in a moment's cowardice she cursed herself for, she'd ducked back out of the light and stood, still and stiff as she could stand, one fist tight against her belly, her back against the shack wall's shaggy bark.

The whole capture quivered before her, leaving her with the anger, the frustration, the outrage you might have at a child or lover snatched from your arms. She watched them ride off with Rahm—and, by starts, hesitations, and sprints, at a safe distance, one street away from the common, she followed them.

Since she had first left Calvicon, Naä had pretty much done as she wanted—within the constraints necessity placed about a wandering singer's song. She was a woman of strong feeling and quiet demeanor. Last night, she'd watched what had happened in the Çironian village, but from the ends of alleys, crouching behind fences, up through the chink in a grain-cellar door, while soldiers and villagers had rattled the boards above her, till one arm broke through, to flail, bloody, about her in the dark, hitting her on the ear and shoulders, while she knelt in the three-foot space below, trying not to make a sound while others screamed above her.

Before sun-up, Naä had climbed quietly out, stumbled over the bodies, and—like Rahm—started from the town.

She had not, however, gone as far.

She walked an hour in the dark, till the salmon-streaked promise of sunrise hemmed the night. She stopped beneath a maple grove, looked down among dark roots squirming at her feet, put her hands to the sides of her head and, breathing deeply, stood awhile, now with eyes opened, now with them closed. A few times, she gave an audible gasp.

Once she shook her head.

Then she took her hands down slowly, to let them fall, finally, against her thighs.

A minute later, she whispered, *"No . . . !"*

Then she turned and began to walk briskly back. At the edge of the burial meadow, she crouched in a clump of brush, while one and another wagon pulled up to the field all through the morning, each accompanied by three or four soldiers, to dump its corpses.

To the sound of creaking cart-beds and thumping bodies, she fell asleep—and woke, hours later, in the hot sun, with a nauseous smell in her nose and a bad taste in her mouth. Looking carefully through the brush, she saw that no attempt had been made to cover the bodies on the grass.

One cart had been left near.

But no one was about.

Keeping to the woods, she went around to the charred ruins of Ienbar's shack. Again, she waited for moments. Then, she pulled her harp around before her, dropped to her knees, tugged aside a half burned log, and dug out a hole for the instrument. With some cloth, burned along one side, she wrapped it. A large rock went over the opening. Then she scattered dirt and cinders on it. Fifteen minutes later, as she kicked away knee prints, footprints, then stepped back onto the grass, she was sure no one would know her harp was entombed there. Walking along the burned foundation, she paused to look back, then beat at the charcoal on her knees and hands, now and again wiping at her smudged face. Just inside, on a log gone gray and black over its burned-away side, the blade discolored near the bone handle with burn marks but the point sharp and the edge bright, one of Ienbar's well-sharpened cooking knives lay. She stepped in, picked it up, looked at it on both sides, then pushed it under the sash at her belt.

Very soon she'd hunted up the site of the Myetran camp.

Hidden in the brush and low trees on a slight rise, Naä watched awhile. She thought hard. When she decided what she might do, she turned back—

And caught her breath.

She let it out again, with one hand at her throat; then, as she recovered herself, touched the tree beside her. "Qualt—I didn't realize you were . . ."

When he dropped from the low branch on which he'd been sitting, she caught her breath again, because he was so loud in the leaves around them. "Naä," he said, though obviously he'd been watching her for minutes, "what dost thou here?"

"The same thing I bet you are. Look," and she turned back to the camp below them. "Those open carts there—can you believe it, they've brought their water in them, over from the quarry. Someone goes to get a dipper of water from them perhaps every five or ten minutes. It would be easy to get behind them and . . . What could you put in them, Qualt, to foul the supply and make the drinker gut-sick . . . ? And—"

The youth settled on one hip, grinning. "Yes?"

"Right over there is the back of their enclosure, where they've put their horses. It's very close to the woods. If I could get some tinder and start some dry weeds burning, I could heave them inside—I know horses, Qualt. They don't like fire. And if they bolted, those railings wouldn't hold five minutes . . . now if there were only something we could do about the prisoners. I think that's the corral where they've got them, way across there. But I don't believe I could get that far without being spotted. There was all this activity there, just about twenty minutes back—"

The young garbage collector nodded, dappled light behind one ear making it luminously red—Qualt had tied his long hair back. "They took many of them back into town—to put them in the council building."

"In the council building?" Naä asked.

"It looked to me as if they took everyone between fifteen and fifty-years-old and decided to put them in the cellar of the strong building. Only the old ones—and the little children—are left out there, in the hot sun."

"You saw them?" she said. "I was here twenty minutes ago, and I couldn't . . . But you saw them—take the prisoners from here, all the way into town and put them in the council building . . . ?"

Qualt pursed his lips a moment, blinking. Then he said: "Come. Thou knowest where my hut is, by the dump?"

"I've never been there. But Rimgia once pointed out the path to it."

Qualt snuffled, grinning; she realized it was a joke when he said: "There—thy nose will tell thee where it is if thou comest anywhere close. Go on—and meet me there."

He turned, grabbed a branch of the tree he'd been perched in and started to climb.

"Won't you come with me, Qualt?" she asked, surprised.

"Go on." He looked back over his shoulder. "Go there. And I'll meet thee." He vaulted up to the next branch. A moment later his outsized feet pulled up among the leaves. "Go on. Don't worry. I'll be there!"

It wasn't a time for questioning. And besides, she couldn't see him any longer, even when she squinted—though she could still hear the leaves and the branches gnashing against one another. Naä started through the trees again.

She couldn't imagine she'd taken much time. When, not half an hour later, she came around the corner of his house, she was as surprised to see him standing in the yard, among his odd and leaning collection of junk, as she had been when she'd turned to see him in the woods.

"Here," he said, with no explanation as to how he'd gotten from one place to the other so much ahead of her. "This is for their water." He picked up the old basket sitting on the moss by his foot. On both the basket edge and the handle, bits of wicker had come loose.

"What is—" Then she wrinkled her face. In the general stink from the proximity of the dump, this stench cut through with distressing putrescence. Leaves lined the wicker. In among them nested something odorous and black—no, a wet green so dark it might as *well* be black.

"Where in the world did you *get* that?" she asked.

Qualt nodded to the side. "Down in the ravine. There's lots of stuff I know about in there. Likely thou mayest get this on thy hands. Thou must wash them well with both soap and salt, before thou touchest thy face or mouth—otherwise, thy guts shall soon run loose as the Myetrans' when this stuff goes in their drink." Qualt handed her the foul basket. "Under the leaves are iron and flint for fire. The cattail fluff that you can get down this side of the quarry lake will give thee lots and lots of smoke—if smoke is what thou wishest."

Behind Qualt stood a much larger basket, brim full, that Naä glanced down at now: millet cobs, some half-eaten yams, a chicken head—

"And any of the dried stuffs from the side of the hill beside the big rocks near their camp will flame up nicely."

"All right," she said. "This should do, I think—at least I hope it will."

There were no thanks. But both grinned at each other. Then, the little basket at her thigh, she was moving off through the woods, making again for the Myetran camp.

Naä was astonished how easily the carrying out of the plan went. Behind one wagon, a handful of slop, up and over the edge—splash—then on behind the next—splash, again; and behind the next. Back under the cover of the trees, she tried out the flint and metal on a bit of the bale of dried brush she'd gathered, repeating to herself as she crouched in the shadow, "It's the idea and not the doing—and having the stuff to do the doing with!"

At the horse enclosure, she thrust five big bales of dried kindling one after the other through the back fence. With crossed spears, way on the far side the two guards looked resolutely in the opposite direction.

She was back in the woods, starting to bring down another bale, when an officer rode up to return a horse to the enclosure—so she waited. Minutes later, she was down on her knees, behind the last bale, beating and beating the iron against the stone, till the oiled rag suddenly caught. A moment later, there was a rush of heat, of crackling, of orange flame—and she was running off again, into the woods. She turned back once, as two horses trotted over to examine the fire, then suddenly reared, whinnied, and galloped away—and do you know, the spear guards *still* had not looked!

She ran faster up the forested hill. Only twenty steps later, when more horses began to whinny behind her, did she hear the first man shout.

A moment later, she was again on her knees, laughing.

She laughed again, about an hour on, when, as she walked among the houses nearer the common, chubby Jallet, Mantice's boy with the cast in his right eye, stopped to tell her what had happened to the soldiers, returning to camp under the trees behind the council building:

"When those bad men went under the stand of trees that are so thick in their branches that they make noon look near night, an old cabbage hit one of them on the shoulder—then eggs and goat offal and chicken heads and other nasty things began to pelt them from up in the leaves—from someone who could aim, too. For one got a splat of shit in his visor and another with his helmet off got cut on the face with a broken pot!"

Still laughing, Naä managed to say: "But it must have been—" Then she caught herself. "It must have been quite a little rain of slop and garbage!"

"It wasn't Qualt," Jallet said.

Naä was surprised that the child's thoughts had gone like hers to the dump. But then, what else would a town person have thought?

"It wasn't anybody at all," Jallet explained, "because the Myetrans got real angry, and began to climb the trees and look about, and there wasn't anybody in them. Nobody had gone up them. And nobody—except the Myetrans—ever came down!"

"I see," Naä said. "So it just . . . happened!"

Jallet nodded, with his unsettling glance that, because of the cast, you never knew where it was fixed. But while Naä laughed, she wondered.

Later that evening, though, when she was passing through the common, she saw four Çironians bound before a group of bewildered villagers. As she stopped to watch, the bored officer in his black hood and immobile cloak announced their crime was "mischief against Myetra! For the crime of which, ten lashes each!" Their hands thonged together before them, their clothes torn from their backs, the woman and the three men shuffled from side to side, blinked, and looked frightened. Were they, she wondered suddenly, being lashed for her misdoings? Or Qualt's? It was the first moment of circumspection she'd had in the heady rush of her mischief. When the first lash fell, little Kenisa, standing next to her and looking very serious, reached up quietly to take Naä's hand—Naä flinched a moment, so that Kenisa glanced up at her. But then, Naä had already gotten the soap and salt and done the obligatory hand-washing earlier at Hara's house.

Several times and very loudly, the sunset curfew ordinance was read out at all corners of the common.

And finally, in full darkness, Naä was still slipping between the houses and along the back paths behind them, contemplating what more she might do to cause the soldiers inconvenience, when she saw Rahm.

For the first minutes behind the horses, Rahm had stumbled and crouched at the end of the rope. Then he just walked, head low and half bent over. Finally he'd come on behind them, the tall, muscular youth Naä knew as Ienbar's helper and her friend—almost as if, bit by bit, he'd put aside some mime of weakness he'd been performing for his captors that they had not even bothered to notice. It's amazing, Naä thought, hurrying on beside, they really haven't looked at him once.

I could run out, take my knife, slash the rope, and the two of us could be free and off in the dark in seconds! She grasped the knife at her belt, finally pulled it loose. But whenever she squeezed the handle, picturing herself sprinting forward, she felt a glittering web of terror, a web flung up between her and the figures moving through the dark streets.

If I surprised him and he *really* stumbled or cried out—

If just one of them *chose* to look back, by chance—

If he—or I—made some *accidental* sound—

This bravery of the body in sight of bodies was a very different act, she realized, from the sort she'd managed earlier, with a camp half asleep under the hottest of the day's sun.

But still, across the little span of night, not one of the soldiers had actually *looked* at him, so smug were they in their superiority! Naä was still thinking this when the soldiers, Rahm bound behind them, returned to the common's edge and started across for the council house. Qualt had been right: the strongest building in the town, now it was being used as a Myetran prison. She stepped out, then stopped as though the stone wall were only feet in front of her instead of catercorner across the square. Naä stepped back into the last doorway, to watch the soldiers and her friend mount the ten stone steps and enter the plank door. Torchlight flickered within. She cursed, cursed again. But there was no way to breach those well-set rocks. She turned among the houses and began to hurry down a back street.

Half an hour later, Naä was again among the dark trees, the Myetran camp before her—though, save a cook fire off over there, or a line of light under the edge of a tent to the right, it was all but invisible. She crossed between the underbrush and a back wall of canvas, that, bellying with the night's breeze, gave a snap, then sagged. Moving closer, she heard a voice within:

"Lieutenant Kire, this will stop! I ordered them executed. You had them flogged."

A softer voice, with a roughness to it almost menacing: "Nactor, my prince—"

"I want no explanations! You, Kire, have been given a great opportunity, an opportunity allowed to few—to lead a brigade of Myetra. Is this how you use your officer's privilege? This is how you'd have Myetra known? Were you not so good a soldier, things would go badly for you now—very badly. It is only your skill at arms that saves you from my anger." There was a pause. "It's dangerous to cross me, Kire. You know that, don't you?"

"My prince, truly I thought—"

"What did you think, Kire? At this point I would like to know if you were thinking at all. Personally, I thought you'd lost your mind. Did you think, perhaps, it was an accident when a fire started in the horse yard? Did you think, perhaps, it was happenstance when most of three platoons came down with dysentery in the same hour?"

"My prince—" The man's breath came stiffly,

hoarsely, uncomfortably in his throat—"all we know is that it was not the villagers I had flogged who did it. What I thought, my prince—I thought we might . . . learn something from them—who is responsible for the fire, the water."

"We could take any one of them from the street and beat that knowledge from him."

"You've tried that, my prince." He drew a loud frustrated breath. "Sire, these are a peaceful people. They don't even have a word for weapons. The tactics we are using here are inappropriate—more than inappropriate: wasteful, of our time and energy."

"Peaceful, are they? If they have no word for them, that just means they will be that much cleverer in coming up with weapons you or I would never think to name as such. There have already been attempts at sabotage—"

"But let me at least try a method that seems, to me, right for this situation. Let me pick out someone, gain his confidence, then send him among them so that we can learn and direct, both. Let me select a man who—"

"Choose a woman." Nactor's voice was hard, almost shrill. "A girl, rather. I am not interested in confidences, Kire. I'm interested in terror, fear, and domination. And she must be terrified of you, Kire—she must know that if she displeases you in the slightest thing, then . . . you will kill her!" (Near Naä's cheek the canvas snapped once more. She pulled sharply back, though more at the indifferent cruelty than the surprise. Again she moved forward.) "Peaceful! If they seem peaceful, it is because we have given them no opportunity to be other-

wise. Peaceful? Ha! Get this woman. Yes—
there are three things you must do to her: bed
her, beat her, and let her know her life hangs
by no more than your whim, a hair . . . a hair
that can break any moment you decide. Then
. . . well, then, use her as you will." (In the
pause, Naä tried to picture the lieutenant's and
the prince's expressions.) "You understand,
Kire: this is an order. Break her, violate her.
Then, when you've done that, you may use her
as you wish for whatever spying—or instruc-
tion—you can. And when we depart here, you
will kill her—like any other soldier finished
with an enemy whore. You've disobeyed me
once, Kire. If you do it again . . ."

Naä heard the sounds of boots, over matting
and hard-packed earth. Canvas scratched
against canvas as the flap was pushed back.
Kire spoke to a guard: "Go into town, Uk. Take
horses and two more men—requisition a portable light from Power Supplies. And bring
back some woman of Çiron—"

The prince laughed: "Go into town and find a
young and pretty one. I really think this should
be rather fun—I'm going back to my tent."

"Obey your prince." Kire spoke to the big
soldier.

Naä realized she was gripping the edge of the
canvas in her fist. Stupid! she thought, and released it, hoping no one within had seen. She
moved back into the darkness.

There—the guard was going toward Supplies.

Naä backed up half a dozen steps, turned,
and sprinted into the trees alongside the drop
that, in the autumn, became a stream—but

was now no more than a marshy strip of leaves at the bottom of the night.

There'd not been much pleasure that day for Uk. In the morning he'd stuck his head out from the warmth of his sleeping bag into mist cut through with birch trees. Squatting by him the tall soldier on clean-up detail, who'd shaken him by the shoulder, said: "Your friend's over there in the wagon—" Uk had been confused enough to believe for a moment the man was telling him Mrowky'd come back—"if you want to see him, before we put him under."

Then, understanding, Uk pushed himself out of the bag to stand in the inverted evening that was dawn. In his brown military underwear, occasionally scratching his stomach, he walked the quarter mile to the casualty wagon.

The men had already finished the grave pit. The wagon detail had found only three Myetran dead around the village—the perfect average for this operation.

"You want his armor?" one asked.

Uk glanced over the wagon's edge, where—with the two other corpses—Mrowky sprawled, hair plastered to his head with mud, mud dried over one side of his face, neck swollen, purple and black, bulging over the rim of his breast plate. Uk started to say he'd take the armor, till he realized he'd have to take it from the corpse himself. "Naw. Naw, you bury him in it. He was a good soldier. He was a good—" Uk turned from the cart abruptly, to start back, thinking: Mrowky was a stupid, lecherous pest, who'd talked too loud and too much.

Was Mrowky a bad man? he let himself wonder. Then, thirty meters from the wagon, out loud Uk said: "Mrowky was the best . . . !" because the concept of a friend seemed somehow such a rare, and valuable, and important thing in the hazed-over dawn by the trees at the edge of this ragged village who-knew-where. He thought (and knew it was true, thinking it): Mrowky would have killed for me. I would have killed for him. . . . There in the wet road, the fact stopped him, struck his eyes to tears, then, moments on, dried them. He took a loud, ragged breath, and walked back among the morning cook fires.

Some hours later, on a patrol through town, when the dozen of them were a street away from the market common, just across from the well, Uk glanced aside to see the redheaded girl, being hurried by her equally redheaded brother up some low steps and through a shack door. And that's the woman Mrowky died for, Uk thought. No, it wasn't fair.

And what about the crazed peasant who'd murdered Mrowky? Would I even recognize him, Uk had pondered, his face once more returned to normal, after that murderous frenzy—?

Later, crossed-legged on the ground, while he was eating his dinner, Uk was called for guard duty at Lieutenant Kire's tent. And the lieutenant himself, on going out, stopped in a swag of black, his cloak a dark tongue thrust straight down behind, to ask in the evening's slant-light: "How's it going for you there, Uk?"

Clearly the lieutenant had heard the others speak of the big soldier's loss. "I'm all right,

Sir," Uk answered—and wondered why even that absurdly small bit of concern made him feel better. Perhaps, he reflected, as, in the east, indigo darkened the village roofs, it's because any and all concern in this landscape—by anyone or for anyone—was so rare.

Only a bit of light lit a few western clouds as Prince Nactor had marched up to Kire's tent flap; when, outside, Uk heard the altercation within, he did not exactly listen to their converse. (That's what Mrowky would have done—then been back to whisper about it half the night . . .) Not that it kept their words from him. But while they'd talked, voices rising and lowering, he tried to move his mind years and miles away, to fix on a stream in his own village, with its dark and muddy bank rich in frogs and dragonflies—

Then light fell in his eyes, and Kire was saying: "Go into town, Uk. Take horses and two more men—requisition a portable light from Power Supplies. And bring back some woman of Çiron—"

Behind Kire, the prince laughed: "Go into town and find a young and pretty one. I really think this should be rather fun—I'm going back to my tent."

Kire said: "Obey your prince."

Surprised, the big soldier threw up his fist in salute.

Minutes later, with two other soldiers, their mounts stepping carefully in the dark, Uk rode off between the last of the cook fires, red and wobbling against a black so intense it was blue. One of the riders, the box holding the illuminating filament slung around his neck, reached down now and clicked it on. A beam of white fanned to the left of his horse. (In the bushes to the right, with twigs pricking her thighs and wrists, Naä pulled back in loud leaves—and stopped breathing.) Clucking at his stallion, while some animal thrashed to his right in the brush, Uk glanced over at the beam. "Douse that. We don't need it."

The light died.

What had been in Uk's mind was that the moon's sliver from the previous night should have grown a bit by this evening. But either the world had moved from crescent moon to moon's dark, or overcast hid all illumination. Probably they could have used a light, Uk decided, as the horses left the smell of burning for the town's dark streets. But that only resolved him, out of whatever stubbornness, not to have it on at all.

Really, he thought, later, it was not so much a conscious decision. Rather, as Uk led the other two soldiers through the night village, at a certain point he simply realized where he was going, what he had already started to do, and let himself go on to do it. The lieutenant had told him to bring back a village woman. What other woman should he bring? He knew where this one lived. If he started looking in houses at random, it could take forever. Between the dark shacks of the village, he let his horse take him out of the market square. ". . . Break her, violate her!" the prince had ordered. Well, he thought, reining to the left, it was only what had already started to happen to her.

In the light from one window, he made out

the well, and turned toward where the door to the house should be—yes; there were the steps. He gave the order to dismount, dropped to the ground himself, stepped up on the porch and, with his fist, hammered on the door.

Then he hammered again.

When he struck the door a third time, a voice within, like a child's, asked: "Yes . . . ? Who—" so that, when light rose up along the crack in the door, he expected the figure standing behind it to be her.

But it was the boy, his hair coppery in the firelight inside, one braid falling in front of his strong little shoulders, one behind.

Uk pushed the door in. "Where's the girl, Çironian?"

Stepping back, the boy said, "Sir . . . ?"

"Where's the girl who lives here . . . your sister?" Certainly in a village like this, she must be his sister.

"What wouldst thou—?"

Surprised at his own impatience, with the heel of his hand Uk hit the boy's naked shoulder. "Call her!"

A girl's voice came, somewhere from within: "Abrid . . . ?"

The boy's fearful face looking up at Uk seemed wholly absurd. Behind, one of the other soldiers moved closer.

The frightened boy called over his shoulder: "Rimgia . . . ?"

In the part of the room that, outside the firelight's immediate range, was shadow, a hanging moved. The girl stepped hesitantly in. The first thing Uk thought was how ridiculously young they both were! Surely this afternoon, when he'd glimpsed them in the glaring street, they'd been older than this . . . ?

Her bright hair, unbraided, was tousled; her eyes looked sleepy—swollen with tiredness? Or was it something else? She came forward, with her face full of questioning.

Uk stepped, reached out, and grabbed Rimgia's arm. Her eyes came immediately awake, as he said: "Come on! You're wanted at Lieutenant Kire's tent."

Abrid said: "Touch her gently or not at all—!"

While the girl said: "Please, let me get my—"

Where the rage came from, Uk didn't know. Really, they were only kids. But he released the girl, turned, and gave the boy the back of his hand, against his cheek and neck. Abrid went stumbling back, and sat down, hard, his head cracking against the wall—sat, blinking, terrified. "I have no patience with a silly boy's playing at being a man!" Uk growled.

Rimgia, who had grabbed a shawl from some peg on the wall, froze where she had started to wrap it around herself.

"Go on!" Uk barked. "Cover yourself, you dirty hussy! If you'd done that last night—" The hand with which he had struck the boy was shaking. What he'd started to say was that the little guy might be alive now! But that was stupid. They'd never known his friend—even the girl. "Come on!"

The cloth went over her head, wrapped down tight on her shoulders. Her blinking eyes were suddenly shadowed by the indifferent print covering her hair.

Uk took her by the arm and pulled her outside, while she kept trying to look back over her shoulder at her brother within still sitting on the floor. "Rimgia—?" That was the boy.

She called out once: "Abrid . . . !"

Which made one of the other soldiers with them grab her and push her further into the dark: "Come on, now—!" which, Uk realized a moment later, might have been to keep him from hitting her; for, at her cry, Uk had raised his shaking hand again.

Why could he not control this absurd anger at these silly, frightened children?

One of the other soldiers gave him the rope when he asked for it. He and the one with the light over his shoulder bound her, clumsily, in the dark; then the soldier who'd pushed her said: "Come, behind the horse—and don't dawdle. If you're thinking about running, forget it. We'll just come back and kill your brother— before we catch you again!"

And a moment later, they were riding through the town, while, now and again, Uk heard—or felt—the girl at the tether's end stumble or, once, cry out.

She'd winced with each of big Uk's barks. She'd bitten down hard as he'd struck Abrid. Now, from doorway to doorway, Naä hurried on beside the three mounted soldiers, with Rimgia going, bound, behind. And Naä thought, as she had thought before: They really *don't* look back.

And then: *Suppose* I did it . . . ?

Fool, she thought. This isn't some ballad or

folk tale about some bit of bird-brained bravery! This is my *life* . . . but, she thought, it's *her*
life too . . .

Then she thought: This time, I *am* going to
do it.

And, as she thought it, she realized she was,
rather, going to do something else!

The web was bound wholly around her now,
glittering against her back, her cheeks, her
calves, her forehead, her thighs. (Let it, she
thought, be an energy flowing into me, not a
draining . . . !)

Naä thought: If I do what I know I'm about to,
I am going to be killed. If I do what I know I'm
about to, I'm going to be . . . I'm going to be
killed—she repeated it in the darkness until it
meant nothing to her. And dashed for the next
doorway. But I have a knife—and so I will kill
one or three or, who knows, even more of
them. Maybe I'll get away. And Rimgia will get
free. That's what's important. That's—

Then, in a movement that was beyond
thought, she sprinted out to Rimgia, reached
the stumbling girl, put one arm firmly around
Rimgia's shoulder and her other hand over
Rimgia's mouth, and kept her pace moving forward. "It's Naä!" she whispered—less then
whispered: mouthed rather, with just the faintest trace of breath, her lips touching Rimgia's
ear; and she was still sure the girl didn't hear.

With her free hand, Naä tugged at the rope,
loosening it, pulling it up to Rimgia's shoulders. In the faintest light from some passing
shutter, Naä saw Rimgia staring at her (their
faces were only inches from each other's) in
terror; yet her head shook a moment, with

some recognition of what was happening. As Naä got the rope free, she glanced toward the horses before her, where none of the men had as yet looked back. *"I'm changing places with you . . . !"* she whispered suddenly to Rimgia.

There was a convulsive movement from the girl, beneath Naä's arm, that, though it was wholly without sound, might as easily have been a laugh as a quiver of fear.

"Go!" Naä went on. *"Get Abrid—take him somewhere out of the village, into the hills, the both of you!"* She had gotten the rope over her own shoulder, when, from Rimgia, still against her, clinging to Naä even though she was no longer bound, there was abrupt movement—for a moment Naä was confused, and frightened, and sure that, in a moment, the whole thing would end. But Rimgia was pushing her shawl over Naä's head, pulling it forward, tucking it down under the rope, now here, now there, all the time half running along beside her in the dark. *"All right!"* Naä whispered, again, in that whisper less than sound.

Now, at once, Rimgia pulled away—or perhaps Naä pulled from Rimgia. Naä stumbled for real, but did not fall. Ahead, the horse to whom she was bound made a corresponding adjustment in his step. And the big soldier astride him—once again—did not turn around to look! Beneath Rimgia's shawl, Naä felt the length of blade at her belt; it seemed small and silly and the idea of killing somebody with it even sillier. Her mouth had gone dry. Her heart was thudding loud enough to make her stagger in her tracks. At least the children might actually get away—

I will be killed, Naä thought once more. But, blessedly, it was still without meaning.

They crossed a stretch that, from the smell and the stubble underfoot, was a burnt field. Fires were burning in the distance. Then other fires were closer. The black-cut gray of birches leaned off into the dark. In front of a tent, the soldiers stopped the horses, dismounted—and, believe it or not, *still* did not bother to look at her!

The big soldier, whose horse she was tied to, pushed back the flap and, leaning within, said: "I've got your girl for you, Lieutenant."

The voice she'd heard before, the one called Kire, said: "Bring her in and leave us, Uk."

Naä clamped her jaw, clutched the shawl tight over her hair, her other hand on the knife hilt under the long cloth, under the rope. Strike, she thought. Who? Which one? Would it be the brutal, vicious soldier who'd struck Abrid and bound Rimgia? Or the lieutenant? Or maybe the prince, if he were still there . . . ? If things had gone this well so far, perhaps it was not so foolish to expect success after all? But she mustn't get cocky. Bravery, daring, courage, yes—but don't abandon common care and sense—though, she wondered, was there anything of sense about this? Remember, she thought, men who do what these men have done are not human, are without feelings, are dogs, are maggots, are worms. . . .

Who will it be first, she thought. Will it be the lieutenant or one of his hulking, beer-gutted guards . . . ?

The big guard, Uk—what a name!—came back and took her arm. As he pulled her into

the wedge of lamplight that was the tent opening, she started to look away, so that he might
not recognize her. Then something made her
stare straight at him.

His heavy featured face was looking directly
ahead, neither to the right nor left. A soldier,
she realized, following orders—doing nothing
more, nothing less. For all his brutality to
Rimgia and Abrid, that's all he was. A pig, a
dog, a worm; and yet as much without will, she
thought, as without sensitivity. He really
doesn't see me at all, Naä reflected. Do any of
them—

"Thank you, Uk. Dismiss the others and return to duty."

And the big soldier, with a fist flung high,
backed through the flap.

The lieutenant stood by the desk against the
tent's striped wall. There was a smell in the
tent that made her recall both the smell in
Qualt's yard and the stronger smell in the
malodorous basket from the afternoon—without its being exactly like either. Was it the mil-
dewed canvas itself? But no, it was a spoiled
scent far closer to animal than vegetable.

Like a black-draped statue, the lieutenant
turned in the light of the lamps, one of
which—a shallow tripodded brazier on a low
table by the cot, where a puma skin, the skull
still in it, had been thrown across the dark
wool blanket (was that what smelled, she wondered)—had a yellow hue: the lamp hanging
from the tent's center by its several brass
chains and the lamp on the desk's corner both
burned with the harshest white fire.

* * *

Outside the tent, Uk stepped to the left of the entrance, breathed deeply in the darkness, spread his legs, put his hands behind his back, taking the at-ease guard position, and thought: There, that's done, however little it was. What am I? A man following orders, nothing more, nothing less. I'm a soldier. Forget this sensitivity. It doesn't become me. Though the night had grown chill around him, there was almost a warmth in the realization, so that, for the first time that day, it seemed he could let his mind drift, let his eyes fix on a bit of light from the tent flaps, that fell on a grass tuft and a flattened stone, while he remembered a stream somewhere, with broken mud, dragonflies, frogs . . .

When the lieutenant looked at Naä, she lowered her eyes, to let the edge of Rimgia's shawl fall as low across her face as it could, even as she thought: but *he* doesn't know what I'm supposed to look like, at all!

The lieutenant walked over to her and pulled at the rope. It was tied so loosely that its two coils dropped down around her feet even as he tugged them once. (There had been three coils when Rimgia had first been tied.) Naä held the shawl closed at her neck more tightly. But he did not seem to think it particularly odd. The feeling that none of them, none of them at all actually saw her, became for a moment a dazzling conviction. I could be anyone here, and it would make no difference—

The lieutenant stepped toward the desk again and turned, his black gloved fingers on some parchments there. A day's beard peppered his cheek.

"Thou lookest to be hard worked," she said shortly, assuming the Çironian idiolect. Her own voice sounded breathless and faint to her. But the words would not stop. "Has doing injury worn thee down?"

He glanced up at her, with a smile which, she realized, looked simply tired. In the brazier's light, his eyes were a smoky hue, as if the irises were circles cut from the undersides of oak leaves, around black pupils.

He said: "I haven't slept much—or well, recently." The oddly hoarse voice, with the carrion odor all around, made her feel as if she'd entered some place more primitive, primordial, and basically lawless than any she recalled from her travels.

"Bad dreams?" Bitterness whetted her voice to a greater sharpness than she'd intended.

Kire walked across the rug, reaching up to push a black pom through a black loop. His hood slipped from bronze hair. It and his cloak dropped to the ground to make a motionless puddle of night, frozen in the moment of its fall. Turning to sit on the cot's edge, absently he felt the prairie lion's skull with black-gloved fingers. Kire's green eyes strayed back to Naä's.

She pulled the shawl tighter; and felt her body tingling with impatience for him to make the move, say a word, give her one reason to lunge with the knife—at his neck. Yes, certainly in the neck. Could she slip beneath the back of the tent? And the stabbing itself—

could she do it so quickly, so deftly, that there would be no noise? Should she wait for him to turn from her? Or should she move closer now—

"You're not a very tall woman," he said, looking up at her. "See over there?" He nodded toward the back of the tent. "One of the ground cords—" and she had the momentarily uncanny feeling that he had heard her thoughts— "at the rear wall has come untied. You can easily slip under the canvas there, if you like— yes, you can go. I have no reason to frighten you any more than you've already been frightened." He gestured to the tent wall. "Go on."

"You want me to *go* . . . ?" she said, dropping the Çironian inflection, but realizing that she had only when he glanced back with raised eyebrow. "Suppose I don't want to. Suppose I want to stay and find out what kind of man you are."

"You're not of Çiron," he said, after a moment. "Who are you?"

"You're called Kire," she said. "My name is . . . Naä. I'm a wanderer, a singer; I'm someone who's come very much to love this place, over which you wreak fire, slaughter, and misery."

What he did next rather surprised her. He lifted the puma pelt from the bed and swung it over his back. She caught a glimpse of its underside, where bits of red and things rolled into black fibres and filaments, only just dried, still clung to the uncured hide. With the motion came a heightened smell—it *was* the source of the stench! The catch under one set of claws, sewn there clumsily with a thong, he hooked to a fastening on the other side of the pelt. Affixed to the Myetran that way, the puma head leered from his shoulder, beside his own.

"Why do you wear that?" she asked.

"This?" He spoke as though the dropping of the cloak and the donning of the hide had been the most unconscious and happenstance of acts. "It was a gift. From a friend. I like it. Cloaks are supposed to blow and ride out behind you on the wind—but ours are too heavy. It takes the glory out of soldiering. This, at least, looks like what it is." With a black glove, he caressed the face beside his own, with its sealed lids, its bared fangs. "And it will remind you, no matter how pleasant I seem, really, I have teeth." (That he might call this odd and smelly space pleasant almost drew a surprised comment from her. But she held it in.) "Come—if you're going to stay, sit here, in the chair—" He indicated the seat at his desk— "where we can talk more easily. Won't you take off your shawl?"

She only held it tighter. But being closer to him would be good. Yes, get closer. She sat in the chair, her knees inches from his.

Yellow fires ran round within the copper rim of the small brazier by his elbow. "You know these people well," Kire said. "Tell me, are they really as gentle as they appear?"

"Yes," she said, unable to keep the challenge out of her voice. "They are."

He smiled: "Couldn't you tell me something small-minded, mean, and nasty you've found among them; or maybe even some overt and active evil: a crippled child teased and made fun of? An old woman's milk stolen from her goat so that she must go hungry, once again—

something that might ease my dreams just a little? Certainly the ordinary pettiness, jealousies, the envy and ire that hold any little town together, beneath the polite greetings and pleasantries in the market square about last week's rain and today's fine weather, must be as common here as they are in any other village. You're a well-traveled woman. You've seen none of the provincial nastiness here that makes the children of such places so frequently loathe their home and yearn to flee somewhere with breathing room, intelligent conversation, and fine music?"

"They've been happy with the music I've brought," Naä said. "And I've been happy with their conversation. I haven't looked for more. And what sort of fool are you—" she looked at him as sharply as she spoke—"that you think the things you speak of could possibly balance the death, the misery, the evil you inflicted here within the hour of your coming?"

He looked back at her, directly. The lion beside him, for the instant, seemed a creature who'd closed its eyes to keep from hearing. A muscle moved in the lieutenant's unshaven jaw. Then he said: "Do you know anything about Myetra, singer? If you visited us, you might be surprised at how pleasantly our farmers and their daughters can dance in a spring evening to the great log drums their wives make in the mountains; or how colorful and cunning the representation of sea creatures and sea plants are that are raised on the tiles decorating the facades of the waterfront warehouses. It's a pleasant place—but there are too many people in it. There is not enough food—

and above all not enough land for our people. It's very simple, singer, what we've chosen to do. It's a plan as clean and as imperative as . . . as a blood drop rolling down a new plastered wall. You see us now taking lives, breaking apart cultures and traditions, here at Çiron, next at Hi-Vator, after that at Requior, then Del Gaizo and eventually at Mallili—finally, even, at Calvicon. But soon what you will see, in a band from water to water, is the growth of a rich, intelligent, and wonderfully hardworking and resourceful people, taking land, making food, imparting their ways and wonders on these myriad backwards folk who have no notion of their own histories for more than five or six generations into the past—the length of time a burial scroll will last before it simply rots away. It's a fine plan, singer. And it inspires the officers above me as well as it inspires the simple soldiers below me."

"And does this plan give you the right to do anything, anything at all—at any level of cruelty and destruction to anyone in your way?"

The lieutenant mused. "There are some among us who think that it does." At every third sentence, the roughness to his voice made her wonder if he weren't drunk.

"And you? What do you think?"

"There are some, both above me and below me, who probably say that I think too much."

In the stench of the uncured hide, within hearing of the burry tones that, really, sounded more animal than human, Naä wondered how anything that anyone might call thinking at all could go on here.

But he moved his forearm, with the black

glove on his hand, along the edge of the desk by the yellow-burning lamp. "Tell me, singer: what would you do if we were in each other's place? What would you do if you wore a stiff black cloak and, despite your love of your home, a sense of injustice—not of justice itself. But, yes, the truth is: I'm troubled at justice's absence—and that trouble stays as close to me as this lion's face is to my own. Would you try to leave, feign sickness, resign your post to another? Or would you stay, mitigating the crimes which those around you commit—changing a death sentence to a prison term, making an execution a flogging, reducing a flogging of twenty lashes to ten? Tell me, singer?"

Naä frowned. Then stopped frowning, and thought: This is perhaps the moment to do it. But the words came from somewhere: "I would get very little sleep." And because these words came too, she said: "If you love your own home, can't you love the idea of home that other people have? That's what a sense of justice is, isn't it? And the plan you talk of, it's not a just one at all. I've looked your men in the face. I've heard your superiors talking. Your men have forgotten all plans and are only faithful to following orders. And all your superiors are after is the power and privilege the plan has most accidentally ceded them! So without justice behind it, or real commitment to support it, what is your plan after that?" The words came, she found herself thinking, like the words to a new song. "Why not turn openly against it? Why not fight it and them until they strip skin and muscle from you, till no muscle moves, till there is no blood left in you to move them—"

"Now—" and she was thinking, will actions come as fast and as easily as those words? when he said—"I should probably smash you across the face with my fist, for daring even to suggest resistance to Myetra." He raised his hand, and the gloved fingers curled slowly in. "And show you why, through sheer force, that is such an absurd notion. But I don't think I shall . . . this time." He looked at her seriously.

Again she felt her whole body begin to tingle. "You mitigate," she said. "You turn twenty lashes to ten. And when you are told to rape, break, and violate, you turn it into talk—"

He raised a bronze eyebrow. "Who told you that?"

"Your guard," she said quickly, "when he was bringing me back from town—those were Prince Nactor's . . . orders, yes?"

"Uk?" The lieutenant looked honestly puzzled. Then, he barked a syllable of laughter. "You're a liar—or a fool! That sort of loose tongue is not Uk's style. Believe me, I know my men. No, we had a guard here, once, who might have said that. But he's . . . not with us now. And what I said to Nactor, I left with Nactor, young lady. Right now, I hate Prince Nactor as he hates me. No . . . I think, perhaps, I will walk you back to the village. We will go together: this way you will have no problems with obstreperous—or loose-tongued—guards." He rose.

And amidst the tingling, she thought—somewhere on the burnt field, somewhere in an alley of the town, yes, when the two of us are alone together, *that's* where I'll do it. Certainly that would be better—

He stood, and reached down for her shoulder. But suppose he binds me again? she thought, as she rose in his grip. Wasn't it better to do it now and have done? (His black-gloved fingers on her shoulder were strong.) Or was hers simply the endlessly rationalized delay of someone blatantly terrified of killing?

"I think," she said softly, "you are a good and thoughtful man."

What she thought was: You are an evil pig a-wallow in a rotten sty!

He didn't pick up the rope as, holding her arm, he walked her by the brazier, the chair, the desk, across the matting toward the tent flap.

Still supporting her, with his other black glove he took the canvas and pulled it back.

Standing just outside, the prince ran his gauntleted hand down one side of his beard, then the other, and said: "Kire, you *are* a fool! '*Hate* Prince Nactor . . .?' *Guards*—" Naä pulled back, as Kire released her arm. A dozen shadowy soldiers waited in ordered formation behind the bearded prince—"arrest Lieutenant Kire—for incompetence, insubordination, and treason! And also the woman—"

The hesitation that had plagued her moments ago vanished before the immediate. Naä dodged behind the lieutenant, lunged for the table, thrust her hand under the brazier, and hurled fire—in a sheet that astonished her, even as it hung a moment in the air, and flickered, and threw up coiling smoke tendrils, a curtain of blue and yellow effulgence, of falling, flaming oil, dropping to the matting, arching toward the striped wall opposite. That same moment she hurled herself to the floor and rolled against the tent's back canvas. Guards shouted. Were any of them dodging around the back? But, yes, and she was under, up in the dark and the cool night, running—mercifully no tree or water barrel stood before her, or she would have smashed into it and knocked herself unconscious.

Naä ran.

Branches raked at her, bushes snatched at and scraped her. Rimgia's shawl caught and tore—Naä paused to jerk it (swallowing the impulse to scream); she pulled free, snatched it after her, and ran again in a chatter of brush and leaves, till she tripped—and went sprawling. What she'd tripped on was large and rolled a little, loudly.

Flies in the dark make an unholy sound—and hundreds of them scritted, disturbed now, from whatever she'd fallen over. She caught the stench—like the puma pelt and the basket and the ravine itself, intensified to gagging, eyewatering level—and pulled herself away.

(She would forever recall it as some villager's corpse, slain and left to lie. Actually, though, it was a prairie lion carcass: the evening just before the attack, Mrowky and Uk had been ordered to dump it in the forest three hundred paces off. But Mrowky couldn't stand the thing and had insisted on leaving it here, *right* now, we've taken it far enough, nobody'll find—no, I *mean* it! I'm leaving it! I don't care what you do. Put the damned thing *down*, I said—now!)

Turning, gasping, Naä saw flames behind

her; between the sounds of her breaths, back
in the camp she heard soldiers shouting.

Another sound: the splat of water tossed on
canvas (with the sound of the last flies settling)—how close she still was! How little
ground she'd covered! And there were soldiers
beating loudly in the brush behind the burning
tent. Naä pushed herself up and ran again. For
a long time.

Qualt's and his companion's mischief had also
continued on, as you surely inferred. At various places about the town and the camp
there'd been four more rains of garbage from
the trees. The one Qualt felt most satisfied
over was when, during the distraction that the
last shower of fish-heads, peachpits, and old
bird's-nests caused, his flying friend, still unseen, had been able to drop two skins of water
into the diamond-wired corral where more
than a dozen oldsters and infants were sitting
or standing, more or less bewildered, in the
burning sun.

But now, with the Winged One, in the darkness, Qualt was once more crouched among
the trees beside the Myetran camp, listening—
rather the Winged One was listening and re-
porting to Qualt what he heard, for they were
too far away from the tent for Qualt to hear directly. Heads bent together in the dark, ear
touching ear, the Winged One related: "He
asks if you folk are as gentle as you appear
. . . She says, yes, you are . . . Now he wants to
know what town secrets, what petty jealousies, envy, and ire she can tell him of; while

she . . . she says you like her music, and she likes what you have to say . . . he tells her what a pleasant place his own home, Myetra, is, and how, after they have crushed Çiron, they will go on to destroy Hi-Vator, Requior, Del Gaizo—"

Somewhat to Qualt's surprise, it was at this mention of Hi-Vator that the Winged One suddenly went a-quiver in the dark. The wind of his sails set the leaves about them shaking and shushing. And one membrane brushed and brushed Qualt's back.

"We must go to Hi-Vator—now, we must go! Don't you think so, groundling? And you can hide there as I have hidden here—and maybe we can even play some tricks as we have played here? But I will tell them of their danger! Though perhaps, after we get there, it would be best if I hid—and you went up to implore the Queen and her Handsman to save themselves; for there are few in Hi-Vator who ever paid much attention to me—and then, most of them, only to curse me. Of course, we could go together . . . and no one who knew the true import of the message I bring could really think evil of me anymore—do you think?"

"Dost *thou* think," Qualt demanded, his hand on the hard, furry shoulder beside him, that flexed and flexed in darkness, "that the Winged Ones there might help us here?"

"Help you?" The beating paused a puzzled moment. "I dare say they could if they wanted. But help you? After all the help I've given you today, carrying you here, getting you there, lifting you out of this danger and away from that one, don't you think it's time, given the gravity of this turn, for *you* to think about helping *me*?"

"Then we must go to thy nest at Hi-Vator! Here, let me mount thee—" and, rising in the darkness from his squat, steadying himself on the shoulder below him, Qualt stepped over and around to the soft dirt behind. The warm back rose against his belly, his chest.

"Hold tight—we have not gone this far before! But you know now how it's done!"

In the black, Qualt clutched the Winged One's neck. Great vibrations started either side of him. Twigs and soft soil dropped away beneath his bare feet. Swinging free, his legs brushed their calves by the Winged One's rough heels.

"But what of the singer?" Qualt thought to call.

"Oh," and the head strained back beside his, "she has already escaped them—and is off running in the woods! There, look—their tent's on fire. And all is confusion with them." And they rose above the trees, Qualt looking down over the furred shoulder, to see flames lapping at the striped wall flare now, then retreat under the slap of water, then surge still again. Beside him, wings gathered up, beat hugely down—

How, Qualt wondered, could such flight be carried on in the dark—even as the first moonlight cleared. Then he forgot the paring of light above and simply clung, sometimes with his eyes closed, sometimes merely squinting against the wind.

They rose before the mountains.

And rose.

And rose—till, beside the rush of water over the rocks, at last Qualt stepped away from his flying companion, arms tingling, oddly light-headed.

"See there—the fire up on that ledge?" the Winged One said, while Qualt tried to catch his breath. "Climb for it, groundling!"

"Climb . . . ?"

"Up the webbing there. See the guy-lines running from under those rocks?"

There was no talk now—and Qualt was glad of it—of either of them continuing alone or either of them hiding.

They climbed the sagging net.

As Qualt passed one ledge, a Winged One, very fat, waddled quickly to the edge and, with lips pulled back from little teeth and little lids squeezed closed, followed them with her face from below to above.

They walked along a stone cliff, Qualt picking his way carefully, lagging further and further behind his companion, who, wings wide, bounded ahead, till three youngsters half ran, half soared from the cave-mouth beside him, to freeze, ears cocked and gawking. At a sudden mew within, they retreated. But now his companion waited for Qualt to catch up, making some disgusted comment about the children Qualt didn't wholly follow.

Steps had been carved into the mountain, that they had to climb. Some of the edges were stone. Some were roots, with earth packed behind them. Qualt moved his hands along the stone walls either side and wondered why his companion, behind him now on the stairs, didn't fly this last length of the ascent—which was apparently not the last length after all, because now they had to climb up another fifty feet of webbing, with the rush and rumble of falling water invisible below among dark rocks.

Finally they gained a ledge where a dozen Winged Ones waited. Qualt was very confused for a while, since no one seemed to want to speak to them.

Fires burned in several stone tubs. The cave entrances flickered and resounded with wings going in and out, with mewing retreating and emerging. Finally, Qualt heard someone say beside him, in that high, childish voice they all spoke with: "But you can see, that is *not* the groundling who was here earlier—that is *not* the one who saved my life. I took him home. He has not returned. They look alike, yes—but not that much alike. Don't you see how much smaller he is?

"And you—" which was addressed to Qualt's companion, who, on reaching the ledge, had suddenly seemed to become indifferent to the whole enterprise and was now sitting on the rocky rim, hanging his heels in space, with his sails drawn in about him and feigning great interest in the night breezes and the night clouds and anything that was not the confused converse behind him. "Well," continued the standing Winged One, who wore some sort of flattened chain around his neck (the only dress or ornament Qualt had seen among them so far), "we certainly didn't expect to see *you* here, just now—"

"Please," Qualt said, suddenly stepping forward, "please—thou must understand. But we *heard* something—!"

At which, with a sudden straightening of his hips, his companion pushed himself off the cliff, dropped into the black, like a feet-first dive into ink, then a moment later rose out of it, into the firelight, soaring now beside them, sailing now above them—with a triumphant hoot that Qualt had *never* heard before!

After that, Qualt and his companion both were given lots of attention.

Naä ran—well beyond the camp, now . . . still waiting for footsteps behind her, wondering at the fact that, somehow, she was still alive, to flee, to run, to escape—from her own absurd and dangerous plan. She took long breaths with her mouth wide, to make as little sound as possible. Ienbar's knife was still in her belt. She still held Rimgia's shawl at her neck—and only an hour later, in the woods at the other side of the village, did she realize that she had gone beyond the town as well. She was going up a slope: this way, she realized, would take her toward the quarry where the stone workers went to hew in the day.

Leave this village, she thought. I am a singer! (In the dark, she clutched the knife hilt till it hurt her hand, till it bruised the undersides of her knuckles, till it stung with the salt on her palm.) I am no woman for this sort of thing, whatever this sort of thing was—killing on the sly, making brainlessly heroic rescues. A bit wildly she thought: I could make a ballad out of what I've already done today and tonight and have the satisfaction of knowing no one will ever believe it! You may have lost Rahm. But you saved Rimgia. Reasonably, you can't do more. So go! Go on—!

Which is when her foot went into the ditch— and with the shooting pain, she turned, she fell. I've probably twisted my ankle, she thought. She got herself free, stepped gingerly on it—it didn't hurt that much. But in ten minutes, or when next she got off it, certainly then the throbbing that precluded walking would begin.

From somewhere, the moon (that, earlier, Uk had expected to light his way into town), rose with its crescent of illumination to light Naä's way through the woods. The underbrush tried to slow her, but she hurried on. Then, at the height of another slope, brush gave way to grasses and trees—one of the pear orchards above the village. She started out across it, still cursing her foolhardiness, and shivering when she thought of the mad-luck that had let her get this far.

She shivered again, though the night had grown warmer—and was of the sort that, any other evening, would have been pleasant.

Between moonlit trees, in a small space a few yards to her left, Naä saw dark forms stretched on the grass. More corpses, was her first thought. Even up here . . . ?

Nothing particularly happened to change her mind; but she decided to go closer. Would it be villagers she knew? When she was a yard away, it occurred to her that they might be sleeping soldiers the Myetrans had stationed—which was when one raised on an arm and whispered,

"Who art thou . . . ?" in a voice that, even as it started chills on her back, she recognized.

"Abrid . . . ?" she asked the shadowed figure.

"Who art thou . . . ?" he repeated.

She told him, "It's Naä!"

The moon had leached all red from his braids, leaving them near the gray they were after his work day in the quarry, so that one could see his father in his face . . .

"Rimgia!" she heard the boy whisper, leaning toward the other sleeping figure. "It's Naä!"

A moment on, Naä crouched between the two youngsters, demanding: "But what are you *doing* here—?"

"Thou saidst I should get Abrid," Rimgia whispered sleepily. "I did. We came here—to hide."

"But they'll find you, if they look for you!"

Rimgia sat cross-legged now, rocking backward and forward a little, clearly exhausted. "Why didst thou come up here?"

"To bring you your shawl," Naä said, shortly. She tugged the printed cloth from her shoulder. It had gotten torn several more times. Naä's legs and arms were scratched; and she was still waiting for the ghost of the pain to reassert itself from when she had gone into the muddy ditch—but that was long enough back so that, if it hadn't started to pain her yet, then maybe she hadn't really twisted her ankle at all. She laughed at the thought that luck could go with you as easily as against (the escape seemed beyond luck; like the luck of being born at all)—and tossed the cloth toward the girl; who simply looked at it, where it landed in the grass, tented in three places on stiff stalks.

Naä said: "It got a bit messed up, I think."
Then, simply, she laughed. "I'm so glad to see
you, girl—I'm so glad to see you both!"

Abrid was squatting now. He said: "Naä, nobody will find us up here!"

"*I* found you," Naä said. "And I wasn't even
looking! You've got to go much further. And
really hide this time. But the two of you, together!"

Rimgia raised both hands to her neck, rubbing. "Naä, how did you get away? What happened—why did you come here? Where are
you going—?"

"Get away? It was dumb luck. What happened? I'll tell you the next time we see each
other. Where am I going? I—" and she stopped,
because she couldn't bring herself to say: I'm
terrified and I'm running away . . .

Then Abrid asked: "Where is thy harp?"

Naä looked down at the knife in her hand, its
blade black as water. For the first time in many
minutes she relaxed her fingers; the pain
bloomed like a hot glow around her fist as her
fingers loosened on the handle. "I . . . I put my
harp away for a while. It's not a time for singing. Look, you two must keep going—you must
get miles from the village. As if you're on a
wander together. And then you must hide, not
anywhere you've ever hidden before. But somewhere new." Slowly, the glow went out. "And
so must I—"

"You'll go with us?" Rimgia demanded, leaning forward now, her eyes, for a moment,
bright in the moon.

"I don't know whether I—"

But then Rimgia's eyes turned away, up toward the sky. Abrid was looking, too.

Like a vast and strangely shaped leaf, a figure crossed the moon. Then another. And then another—going in the other direction. A cloud's tendril touched the crescent. Another flying form swooped below it.

"They scare me," Abrid said, dropping back on his buttocks, his crossed feet coming down loudly in the grass. He hugged his knees in tightly, looking up. Half a dozen of the creatures moved in the sky. He spoke in a whisper. "Everyone's always been afraid of them . . ."

"Dost thou think they can see us?" Rimgia asked. "There're so many frightening things around—I've heard of creatures which can weave a man into a web and suffocate him; and lions that roam the level lands; and the Winged Ones—"

"I wish thou wouldst sing a song for us now," Abrid said.

"I don't have my harp," Naä said shortly. "And the Myetrans, I'm afraid, have stolen my voice for a while."

Again she looked at the knife. Again she looked at the sky. "You two," she said, "at least get out of the orchard here and back somewhere in the woods. And hide! I have to go—"

"Where art thou going?" Rimgia asked, now on her knees, now rocking back to get her feet under her. She stood.

"I think," Naä said, "I'm going back to town. Again."

"Naä—?"

For the singer had abruptly turned.

She turned back again. "Yes—?"

Rimgia bent to pick up the shawl. "Thank you!"

"For going back?"

"For trading places with me!"

Naä laughed. Then she started again through the trees. If they've stolen my voice from me, she thought as she entered the woods to descend the slope, I must steal something from them in return. But what can it be that they'll sorely, sorely miss . . . ?

Qualt was in love with Rimgia.

We've written it; it was true.

Thus it would be silly to believe that in the course of all Qualt's enterprises, she was never once in his mind. But it would be equally simplistic to think she formed some sort of focus for him—that somehow, all his acts were envisioned, performed, and evaluated with her image bright before him—that they were done *for* her. Rather, the sort of social catastrophe which Çiron had undergone takes selves already shattered by the simple exigencies of the everyday and drives the fragments even further apart, so that the separate selves of love and bravery, misery and despair, run on a-pace, influencing one another certainly, but not in any way one.

As such catastrophes occasionally evoke extraordinary acts of selflessness or bravery, they sometimes evoke extraordinary efforts to make one part of what is too easily called the self confront another part.

Naä had found Rimgia doubtless because she was not, in that final dash through the woods, looking for her. But once he had conveyed the gravity of what his winged companion had overheard to the Handsman and—a few minutes later—to the Queen at Hi-Vator, Qualt decided with the same force of will which had impelled him for the whole of the day, even to this height, that he must now find Rimgia and speak to her.

Perhaps Qualt's failure—his only failure, really, among all he'd attempted since the Myetrans came—was because he was so certain he knew where to find her.

The scrabblings on the roof were the footsteps of one Winged One, or three, or perhaps more. On the ground beside the hut, light from the crescent moon was lapped and loosed by a score of beating, crossing, conflicting wings.

Someone, unthinking, mewed.

Someone else went, "Shhush!"

Then Qualt lowered himself down from the roof's edge, feeling for the window, the toes of his right foot catching on the shutter's planks—while the night air that, minutes before, had been a torrent around him, was just a breeze at his back. When he swung his other foot against it, the catch gave and the shutter swung in. Stepping about and finding purchase on the sill, he caught the fingertips of his right hand over the upper lintel, and let himself down, till he was sitting in the window, holding onto the beam above with one hand and the window's side with the other, his head—along with both legs—thrust into the darkened hut.

Recalling the motion with which his companion had pushed himself off the upper ledge into the night, Qualt jumped forward—and landed in a squat that dropped him low enough to scrape the knuckles on his right hand painfully on the floor—while his left hand flailed out; because the floor was closer than he'd thought.

Regaining his balance, he whispered: "Rimgia . . . ? Abrid . . . ?" He stood. "Rimgia . . . it's me, Qualt!"

The darkness across the room to his left he recognized as the fireplace—its embers dead. There, next to it, that must have been Kern's pick. And that was probably Kern's—or Rimgia's—fishing pole, against the wall.

"Rimgia . . . ?" He took another step across the kitchen, feeling suddenly the emptiness of the house as the noises on the roof lifted his eyes, but brought forth no sound within.

Didn't Rimgia sleep in the back, over there . . . ?

He pushed the hanging aside and stepped inside. From a half-open shutter, night-light from the moon lay over a pallet bed, with a wrinkled throw across the matting—not unlike the one he so rarely slept on these summer nights in his cottage down by the dump. "Rimgia . . . ?" And Abrid's sleeping space just beyond the wall . . . "Abrid?" He said that out, full voice, three times. Then he said again, more softly, "Rimgia?" He stood there; and while the hanging swung behind him he pulled his lower lip into his mouth, to press it with his front teeth—till, at sudden pain, he let it free, and put his tongue up over his upper lip now. He rubbed both forearms against his ribs—and swallowed; and coughed; and swallowed again. The chill aloft on the night had been refreshing; but its memory made him want to hug himself in his desire for warmth. A vision he'd had, during the whole of the flight down, was of coming in (through the window, more or less as he'd done), to kneel on one knee by her bed, to reach out and touch her shoulder as she slept; then, when his touch startled her awake, so that she lifted her head, pulling copper hair over the pillow (the moonlight was supposed to be full silver, not just this gauze of half-shadow), he would say . . . Qualt took another breath, stepped forward, dropped to a squat, knees winging up beside him, and reached for the bed. He only rested his wide fingers on the wrinkled throw, however—while he tried to take in the fact that she was *really* not here.

Still, if she were absent, it was *her* absence. And everything hers was, it seemed, extraordinarily important at this moment.

"Rimgia," he said, "I like thee—like thee a lot! Dost thou like me? I mean . . . *really* like me?"

Then, because of the scrabbling above, Qualt was up, into the other room (to flee the vacant house that had just held his bravest act that day), to vault onto the sill and twist about, reach up for the lintel, his broad feet—a moment later—disappearing above it.

CHAPTER
SIX

W hat's going to happen to him, do you think? They're gonna kill him?"

Uk said: "Executed at dawn—that's the prince's order."

There was a grunt in the darkness. "Pretty rough on the lieutenant."

Uk said: "About as rough as it gets." He chuckled. It was a dry, dreary, unfeeling chuckle—one he'd started coming out with to make himself seem less feeling than he was. Now, he noted, he did not, indeed, feel much.

"He was a good officer, Lieutenant Kire," another voice said, from the dark on the other side. (No one else had laughed.) "He was always fair."

And another: "He was the best."

"He was a damned good officer," Uk said. "It's too bad—but I guess I understand it. I don't like it. But I understand it."

"Sabotage? Incompetence—treason? You think the charges are fair?"

"I don't know," Uk said. "I don't know if anything in this war is fair—or unfair. But I was standing right out there, with the prince, when the lieutenant was in there talking to her—he's in there, telling her how he's been disobeying orders, trying to make things easier on the villagers, making a flogging of ten lashes into two, things like that. She's supposed to be a prisoner, and he told her right out she could leave if she wanted. I heard him."

"Well, he was good to us, too—and he tried to be good to them, where it wouldn't hurt. It doesn't sit right with me, executing a man 'cause he's fair-minded."

"Naw," Uk said. "It don't work like that."

"How is it supposed to work then! What do you mean, it don't work that way?"

"That's how I thought it worked, too—when I first got here," Uk said. "We'd come into one of these places, hacking up the locals—and I'd think, just like you: it's like swatting at flies with a swatter. Everyone you hit goes down—dead! This isn't fair. So one time, I started pulling my sword swings, aiming for the arms and legs, rather than the neck or the gut. But then I saw what it looked like later—the ones who didn't die right off. And that was awful—the time it took and the pain it took for them to die anyway. I was walking around, looking at all these people, not dead—but half dead. Half dead's a *lot* worse than dead, when you know you're gonna die in another three, six days no matter what anyone does. No—if the lieutenant wanted this war business over, the way to end it is to go in there, fight as best you can, as hard as you can, and get it over as fast as you can. That's how it works. Holding things back, holding things up, slowing things down—that doesn't do any good for anyone. Not for the villagers—and certainly not for you and me. He was just making it longer and harder for us—and the longer and harder it is for you and me, the more chance you and me got of getting killed. No—I liked the lieutenant. He never did anything to me personally; I'm sorry it worked out this way for him. But if I can understand it, he should've been able to figure it out, too. He's an officer."

"Now that's common sense speaking there, Uk," a soldier said, from the dark.

"Sometimes, I think Uk is the only one in this outfit with any common sense at all," another said.

"That means I'm talking too much," Uk said. "Go to sleep now. We have to get up early."

"You mean we got to go see it, like that other time? Aw—good *night!*"

"The lieutenant's really going to be executed?" asked still another, younger, troubled voice.

"That was the order, boy." Grunts and shushings came as a soldier slid further down into his bag. "Now go to sleep."

Rahm sat in the corner, looking over the dark figures who slept, crowded together on the council-cellar floor. A dozen feet away, Gargula was breathing loudly and irregularly; he'd worked on this foundation with Rahm. Old

Brumer leaned his shoulders against the wall, head nestled down in his near-bushel of a beard: he'd been their foreman. Now all of us, Rahm thought, are prisoners here. At the tiny window, just beneath the ceiling, gray had nudged away a corner of black, enough to silhouette the stems outside. Small leaves shook with a breeze.

Then the door creaked.

Someone looked up. Two turned over without looking. Between two black-caped officers, with a regular soldier behind them, a bearded man stepped in. One officer carried a light-box, that, now, he flipped on. A harsh filament glowed white. A fan of light put harsh blacks on the far side of the two dozen sleepers about the floor.

"Well, we have some men in here," said the bearded Myetran. He wore one brown leather gauntlet. His other hand was bare. From some time that seemed at once impossibly immediate yet long ago, Rahm recognized the man who had ridden his horse on the common, who'd spoken into the silver rod—who had burned down Kern. "For a moment, I thought this was the women's holding cell. Lord, it stinks in here!" (A depression in the far corner was full of urine and feces; but it had long since overflowed, to wet almost half the floor.) The man took a few steps—over some sleeping figures. "I have a job for one of you. For a good and lively dog. A strong dog—you, perhaps. Or you . . . ?

"A bunch of dogs, you are?" The man ran a hand down his beard, to pull it back from morning wildness. "Dogs are vicious—they fight one another, tear at one another over the leavings. What I see here is a bunch of simpering monkeys, crawling maggots without the strength to get up off their bellies. Is there someone here that can do a job that needs a man?" He reached aside for the lightbox hanging around the black-cloaked officer's neck to turn its beam toward the floor. "Have you ever killed?"

Eyes squinted; a hand raised to block the glare.

"Why did I waste the question on such a child!" The beam moved on. "Have you, old man, ever taken another's life?"

The old man, coughing twice, seemed bewildered.

"What about you—you look like a strapping fellow. Have you ever killed?"

In the beam, Rahm did not even lower his eyes.

"Come—give us a 'yes' or a 'no'."

Rahm breathed out—dropped his head and raised it.

"Well—have you, now? I wouldn't have thought so, from your eyes. Or then, perhaps I would . . . Get up! Come with me."

Rahm's hips ached; Rahm's knees hurt; his back was stiff—he pushed himself up, one palm behind him on the rough rock—from sitting the night long, almost without movement.

"Come, this way. To the door."

Rahm came slowly, lumbering really, feet seeking bits of bare stone between the bodies. Once he stepped on the hand of someone who woke, grunted, and jerked away. Toward the ground, Rahm mouthed syllables without sound that, had they had it, would have been an apology.

"That's right, Çironian. Over here."

When they were outside in the basement hall, Rahm realized how strong the stench was within, as the door closed behind him—and fresher air struck, hard enough to make him, for a moment, reel.

"I am Prince Nactor. I do not want to know your name; at least not until you have done what it is I need you for. Then, when it is time to reward you, for doing your work well—I *trust* you will do it well—then I'll ask you. And we can celebrate who you are." Tucking his beard back under his chin, the prince turned to the steps. Starting up, he glanced over his shoulder. "You understand, if you do *not* do it well, you will be killed. And there will be no need for anyone to know your name ever again. Tell me, Çironian, can you handle an ax?"

Surrounded by soldiers, Rahm followed. "I can swing a quarryman's pick."

The prince glanced back again. "Likely that will do."

In the building's ground-floor hall, again holding his beard back, the prince stopped to lean close to Rahm. "Aren't you curious about what this work will be?"

"Thou wilt tell me, in thy time."

Nactor chuckled. "And the time is now." Faint orange lay along the windowsill, left of the door. "I need an executioner. I wish to show a treasonous man—and I wish to make it the *last* thing I show him, the last thing that he will ever see—just how gentle and peace-loving you Çironians are."

Against the far wall sat two women prisoners, one of whom, Rahm realized with a quiet start, was the woman with whom he'd first pursued his earliest, happiest, most single-minded sexual explorations; the other was a woman who, during that same summer, had hated him roundly, loudly, adamantly: for she kept a small set of beautifully tended fruit trees beside her house, which he had taken to pillaging, more for the pleasure of her stuttering outrage than for the fruit. (That, he'd simply handed out among his friends.) It had been only Ienbar's threat of a switching that had finally moved him on to other mischief. Indeed, for a while he'd wondered why his relation to either of the women—one was asleep now; one looked dully across the room and did not seem to see him—had not netted him more, the start of a family in one case or, in the other, the reputation as a troublemaker that, had it gone far enough and the elders' council in these very halls received enough complaints, could have gotten him, after a short public trial, turned out of town—at least that was the rumor. In his own memory, he'd never known it to happen. . . .

Of the two soldiers standing near the women—guarding them apparently—one was shaking his head and grinning over something the other had just said.

On the other side of the hall, in a black cloak which, in knife-edged folds, hung to the flagstones, an officer crossed quickly toward the door and, with the heavy plank complaining behind, left.

"I also want to show *you* something," the

prince was saying. "I want you to see—and to tell all around you, once you've seen it—how strict we are with our own. Thus, you'll likely maintain a more realistic picture of how little in the line of mercy you can expect for yourselves. Come this way, now."

A soldier reached over to tug open the door for them—creaking, as Rahm had heard it creak a hundred-fifty, five-hundred-fifty times, three years ago, coming in and out as a workman. Now the sound was alien. Rahm stepped out, and looked up among the few branches, where, near summer's end, brown leaf-clutches were scattered through the darker green.

Here and there, set irregularly toward the common's corners, stood some five of the spidery structures that were the Myetrans' movable light-towers: a great illuminated lamp on one, as Rahm looked at it, went dark, like the rest.

Above it in the sky's lavender-layered gray, something moved.

Rahm frowned.

Four, six, ten of the Winged Ones passed above in a pattern that dissolved and reformed further away; and dissolved again—a pattern that was no pattern.

"Bring the block and the ax!" the prince called. Then his voice returned to conversational level: "You are going to cut off a man's head. That shouldn't be too hard for you—and since he's one of ours, who knows: you might enjoy it."

Still squinting from his sweep of the sky, Rahm looked at the bearded prince beside him.

Rahm's nod was not intended to mean agreement, only to register he had heard. But, from the smart move the man gave—signaling to someone halfway across the grass—Rahm realized, without particularly marking it, agreement was how the prince had taken it.

Across the common, soldiers stood—at attention, in three rows.

"You can bring the prisoner out," the prince said to one of the several soldiers accompanying them—who turned and hurried across the common. The grass, with the few trees here and there on it, seemed to Rahm as oddly unfamiliar as the creaking door to the council house.

They started down the ten stone steps and across the gravel toward where grass took up again. The common at evening was a familiar place. But the common at dawn—when was the last time he'd been here at this hour? Certainly it was more than three years ago. Maybe four or five. If only because all the shadows were pointing in the wrong direction, it might have been a public square in a wholly alien town.

In the back row, two or three soldiers glanced at the sky, then brought their eyes back to the field.

More than a dozen of the Winged Ones turned and turned, infinitely high, infinitely small, infinitely distant.

By two poles, four soldiers carried a large block onto the grass. It looked black and old, at least down to its base; there it was a little lighter. Another man was coming toward Rahm and the prince, carrying an ax by its handle— the double blade hanging before his knees—

his small steps, high chin, and pursed lips attesting to its considerable weight.

Rahm took it in one hand.

The soldier who'd carried it did *not* take a heaving breath; but when Nactor dismissed him, he threw up his fist, turned, and walked heavily back across the field.

The ax *was* heavy. Rahm brought it slowly before him, lowered the blade to the ground, and put his second hand on the haft.

The four soldiers had lowered the block.

"Bring out the prisoner," Nactor said.

Beside them one of the soldiers halloed across the common: "Bring out the prisoner!"

A beat later, some of the Winged Ones swooped, swooped, and swooped again—without, as a group, getting any lower. Then they went back to their lazy flight.

"You will have no trouble with this ax, Çironian. That I can see. At my command, you will cut off the prisoner's head. Do it cleanly, with a single cut. We do not need unnecessary mess, cruelty, or pain. I am very fond of this man. But since he has to die, I want him to die swiftly. You understand me . . . ?"

Rahm nodded. He did not see which of the houses on the common, commandeered by the Myetrans, the prisoner was led from—for at that moment, with the prince's signal, another soldier stepped up beside him. The world blinked out—then reappeared through eyeslits in the black cloth hood dropped over his head.

Rahm looked about.

The cloth tickled his collar bone.

The prince touched Rahm's shoulder, nodded ahead.

Six soldiers walked now with the tall man among them toward the block. Rahm blinked to realize the man—who wore black—was not bound. Only a black cloth was tied around his eyes, though this one was without eyeslits.

Rahm leaned to ask the prince, softly: "Why is he not tied?"

"When we execute common soldiers, we bind them," Nactor said, as softly to Rahm as Rahm had spoken to him. "It's Myetran custom to let our officers die like men. Come."

Across the prisoner's chest, two puma claws were fastened one atop the other, from the pelt he wore around his back.

Inside the hood, Rahm frowned—and hefted up the ax. With the prince and the several others, he started across the grass toward the block. Even without his officer's hood, Rahm recognized him. Rahm's stomach went cold and heavy with that recognition—as if all at once he'd eaten to bloatedness.

When the prisoner raised his hand—to adjust his blindfold or scratch his chin or whatever—a guard struck Kire's hand down viciously; and three more guards seized both his arms, even as no one in the group broke step.

Rahm's hand tightened on the haft. Inside the cloth, his breath whispered.

As they reached the block, a soldier near Kire suddenly kicked him behind his knees, so that he went down. Immediately two others grabbed him, kneeling beside him on one knee so that they could hold him. Two others held his legs. Still two others steadied his shoulders. Kire's head, mouth, and jaw, cut off from bronze-colored hair by the black blindfold, lay left cheek down on the scarred block.

Beside Rahm, the prince sighed.

Rahm looked down at the puma's pelt across Kire's back. The beast's skull had been pulled aside, as if in some scuffle, so that it hung askew.

Inside his hood, without sound, Rahm mouthed: ". . . *friend Kire* . . ." lips brushing cloth.

Beside Rahm, the prince said: "Lieutenant, you will now see just how gentle and peace-loving your Çironians are." He bent down, reached down, thrust a finger beneath the blindfold, and pulled—not gently. With the tug, Kire's head slid inches across stained wood. As the cloth slipped free, the lieutenant grunted. "Look here, now—a nice, gentle Çironian is going to cut your head off." The prince stood up.

From the block, the lieutenant glanced up, green eyes gone near gray with dawn and fear.

There was no recognition in them. But why would there be, Rahm thought, inside his hood.

The prince turned to Rahm. "Kill him—now, Çironian."

Rahm took a step to the side, spread his legs, slid one hand forward on the haft, and hefted the blade over his head. A breeze flattened the cloth to his face, so that any of the guards, looking up, might have seen, under the black, the form of his lips, strained apart with effort.

On the block, Kire pulled his shoulders in. His own lips parted while his eyes squeezed tight, as if by not seeing it he might delay the stroke. His bronze hair was stringy.

The breeze moved it.

Then Kire blinked rapidly three or four times, as if eager for a sight of the morning, the grass, the men around him, even the stained wood obscuring the vision in his lower eye.

The breeze ran in puma fur, parting the hairs to show their lighter roots.

And Rahm brought the ax—not down, but in a diagonal that became even more acute with a twist of his body.

Prince Nactor did not scream, but rather looked down—and staggered—at the ax blade sunk inches into his chest. Rahm yanked the handle, now one way, now the other, as his hands, his shoulders, and the cloth on his face wet with what spurted. As the prince fell, Rahm jerked the ax loose and swung it back around, the blade's side crashing against two of the heads of the guards holding Kire. The swing took it all the way, so that it struck another man and sent him sprawling. Then up, then down—honed metal cut into, and severed, the arm of the officer standing with them, who alone had had the presence to reach down and unsnap his powergun sling—the first man to scream!

Rahm turned again with the ax—one of the soldiers was going backward on his knees, lots of blood on him that wasn't his. Rahm's next chop took off most of a hand—not Kire's—on the block edge. There *were* shouts now. Rahm dropped one hand long enough to rip off the hood and fling it from him over the grass: "Hey, friend Kire, do you know me now? Do we show them, now—?"

Again with both hands on the handle, Rahm pulled the ax free, leaving a gouge on the bloodsplattered hardwood.

The heart-hammering paralysis for Kire ended with the Çironian's voice. The soldiers had all released him—one was running, turning, pulling out his sword as he danced backward; now he began to feint forward.

And Kire crawled, scrambled, clambered around the block and under the swinging blade. A moment later he came up with, first, Nactor's powergun and, a moment after that, in his other hand, the other officer's.

There was still a desperate string of seconds when the lieutenant seemed uncertain if he should fire on his own men—who'd been about to kill him—or obliterate this Çironian madman who was now wreaking mayhem and death among men who, till a day ago, had been his own guards. Finally, when another soldier started toward them, sword drawn, Kire, still on the ground, turned and fired, destroying most of the man save one leg, in a swirl of black smoke and red flame. But it was only then that Kire, glancing up, realized who the marvelous madman was.

Afterthought would have certainly made Kire's decision self-evident. But to some of the soldiers watching, especially from the second and third rows, it seemed—for those moments—as moot and, for the moments after it, as illogical as anything else that had happened in what was still no more than a dozen seconds.

That illogic held them—Uk was one—fixed.

Someone in an officer's cloak had started to run—not toward the mayhem around the block, but toward the soldiers, whose ranks, with each blow and hack and thrust before them, became looser and looser, as some (around Uk) stepped forward and others (in front of him, knocking against him) stepped back.

Crawling on his knees at the end of a swath of bloody grass, doubled over in a kind of moving knot, the officer with the severed arm was *still* screaming. The flap at the crawling man's waist bobbed above his empty sling. His scream seemed at last to move—though very slowly—people about the common's edge.

As, with the powergun in his right hand, Kire dispatched another Myetran and, with the one in his left hand, fired wildly, Rahm paused a moment with his ax, drew a great breath, turned his face to the sky, and shouted, "*Vortcir . . . !*"

He did not shout for help. The young Çironian meant by it only: I am here. See this now and behold me . . . before I die! (For such actions as his—just as much as Naä's—cannot be undertaken other than in the certainty of death.) As such, it was a far more desperate cry than any call for aid. Probably no one about the common's rim understood its meaning: but a chilling combination of triumph and desperation rang through it.

* * *

His own powergun drawn, the officer who'd
run up to the observing soldiers shouted: "Get
in there and stop that—take them down! Go
on! Stop it! Forward! Now!"

Perhaps a third of the soldiers began to run
forward, some pulling their swords loose from
their scabbards as they sprinted across the
grass. Looking for a clear spot between them
for some sort of shot, the officer, shaking his
head, trotted behind them.

At the center of the fray, which had turned
both Kire and Rahm by this time toward the
council building, Rahm's ax sank into another
shoulder; and, as he lugged the blade back, he
gasped: "You see, friend Kire? You see how
peaceful I am—!" And swung the ax again.

RAHM! KIRE—TURN AROUND!

The thunderous voice crashed against the
air itself. The sound staggered all about them.
Every man on the field halted a moment—
except Kire and Rahm.

Turning, Rahm saw the light tower beside
the council house. Halfway up its ladder of
beams and girders, a woman—it was Naä—
crouched in an angle of metal, clutching a
small silver rod.

LEFT, RAHM—DUCK!

Rahm threw himself to the left and to the
ground as smoke and flame burned through
the air above him. Someone who had not
ducked, screamed—very briefly.

BEHIND YOU, KIRE!

From the ground, as he pulled his ax to him, Rahm saw Kire whirl and fire—obliterating two soldiers and causing half a dozen more to scatter.

Because he was on the ground, Rahm looked up—and saw, suddenly, the great forms dropping from the sky. Near the edge of the common, he realized, half a dozen Winged Ones fought with half a dozen Myetrans!

Rahm scrambled to his feet, and swung up the ax with one hand, so that the blade rose over his head, gleaming red and silver.

For Uk, all this—execution, rebellion, the voice from the tower—had played out like a fatigued dream. At the point the officer shouted, "Forward!" he was actually running the thought through his mind: In the morning, I must get up, march to the common, and, with the others, observe the lieutenant's execution. So this is surely some wild night vision which will end, in a moment, with a breath of cold air through the opening of my sleeping bag and the smell of morning gruel.

But, in the real world, such thoughts do not linger. And when, at the "Forward!" order, other soldiers started toward the fray, Uk unsheathed his sword and started too. He'd gone two dozen steps, cutting the distance between him and the wildly fighting figures by a third, by two thirds, when he saw the berserk executioner swing his ax high—Uk had not even seen the hood thrown free. But that was not black cloth wrapped about his head. It was hair, swinging. And the naked face—

Between them, Uk saw Nactor on his side, one hand above his head, the blindfold still looped on three fingers, one eye wide, one closed, and drooling blood. Uk looked up again and recognition hit. It chilled him, turning all possibility of dream into the nightmare whose specific horror was that it took place in one's own bed, in one's own room, in one's own house, in a world that was, indeed, supposed to be precisely his. If, in fact, he had dreamed some beast had, howsoever, been thrust with him into his sleeping bag, and he'd waked to find it clawing and biting at his unarmored belly and unhelmeted face to get free, it would have been exactly as frightening as the realization that this incarnation of evil, who had wildly and insanely murdered Mrowky, was now wreaking death and murder (an arc of blood followed the Çironian's ax blade through the air) among the dozen men around him!

Uk was terrified; but he was also a brave soldier; moreover, he was an intelligent one, which meant he'd already had several occasions to learn that terror in battle—a different thing from ordinary rational fear—had best be moved into and through, so that you came out the other side as quickly as possible—if it were at all possible. That, indeed, is what bravery, military or otherwise, was. Uk took a great wet breath, that had a lot of noise in it—much like a sob, had anyone heard it among the shouts and shrieks. (The damned traitor of a lieutenant was on one knee, firing to the right. Would Kire's beam be what cut Uk down? No matter.

This other one had to be stopped—had to be!)
Uk crouched, his sword back for the thrust,
and ran forward, hammering the ground with
his boots, gasping air, one fist pumping at his
side, the other, holding his sword, awkwardly
poised, his whole body aimed for the space between the backs of two soldiers who were already feinting at the ax-wielder with their
blades.

RAHM! THE ONE COMING UP
ON THE RIGHT OF—!

Rahm swung his ax, and one of the feinters
dove aside and rolled away. The other danced
back. And Rahm saw the big soldier, crouched
low, coming at him—for an instant.

It was a very long instant, though.

Beneath the helmet's rim, the soldier's eyes,
as gray as stone, seemed only a moment away
from magma red. The effort that twisted the
face (the soldier's teeth were bared), seemed to
Rahm an image of absolute, blood-stopping
evil.

Recognizing it, Rahm felt himself lose purchase with his right foot on the grass and earth
that had grown so black and slippery. The
part of him that knew how his own blows
were timed, saw, as clearly as if it had been
written out on one of Ienbar's scrolls, that the
only back-swing he could get in would not con-
nect with any vital part—maybe knock aside
the running man's forward arm, if that. This
mad creature—who had started to holler

now—would collide with him, surely cut him, and likely stab him and stab him and stab again . . .

Then something fell between them—ropes? But they were moving, Rahm saw, backward, away from him. Rahm glanced left and right. The ropes—tied together in some sort of net—had taken several others of the soldiers, too.

If a big man runs head-on into a rope net, the net should give some—two feet, three feet, maybe even twice that. The berserk soldier was no more than five feet from Rahm when the net caught him and started sweeping back.

The big soldier hit those ropes as though they were solid. His free hand grasped a cord near his head. His sword arm went directly through, between thick strands. If you were a wall, and someone ran smack against you, that's the only other way you'd ever see that expression on a man's face: the jaw-jarring jerk—when his chest hit—shook Uk's whole body. The sword flew forward from his hand—Rahm winced to the side, slipping more.

But the blade went clear of Rahm's right hip, by a palm's width—before it slid, spinning, back from grass onto gravel. Rahm reeled again—but kept his balance.

Winged Ones—fifteen, twenty of them, or more—pulled the vine web back across the common. Soldiers stumbled back behind it. At the sides Winged Ones ran with it. At the top others flew with it. Some cords in the web were of a lighter color than the rest; and from the way some soldiers within were struggling to pull one loose from a face or an arm or a leg, Rahm realized in a strangely attenuated knowledge, *those* lines were cave-creature filaments! The Winged Ones at the net's top now descended, making the web a cage. Within were at least twenty-five Myetran soldiers. And the Winged Ones had their own, strangely gripped blades—

". . . Friend Rahm!" It was not Kire's voice, but a familiar mew.

Gasping, Rahm turned to see, like a huge and moving shadow beside him, wings spreading, beating in dawnlight—

". . . Vortcir?"

"Jump on, friend Rahm!"

While the wings turned before him, Rahm dropped the ax and staggered forward. He threw himself at the furry shoulders, caught himself. As they lifted, he called out, sliding, holding his breath then letting it all out: ". . . Vortcir! I cannot hold thee—!"

"Of course you can!" declared the Handsman. And he banked, so that they moved in a far gentler rise; and Rahm, pulling himself forward on his friend's back, sucking in exhausted gasps, looked over Vortcir's shoulder. They sailed left, swooped around, then sailed right, then left again, gaining only a dozen feet each sweep. Wings labored either side of Rahm, as Vortcir circled and circled the common.

On the ground, with their long blades, Winged Ones were not being kind to the soldiers under the net. But Rahm's eyes fixed on the lieutenant.

Kire stood, head hanging and powergun pointed straight into the air. He looked as exhausted as Rahm felt. Slowly Kire's arm went down—and his head rose—so that the gun was pointed at the Winged Ones fighting around the netted Myetrans. There were far more Winged Ones about than Myetrans . . . !

KIRE, NO—!

(Vortcir's translucent ears jerked. Beneath Rahm, the jerk went through all of Vortcir's body, as if it were a moment's pain.) Kire's arm dropped to his side. Then his gloved hand, with the gun, started to rise again.

KIRE!

(Vortcir's ears flicked.) The gun dropped again.

And over Vortcir's shoulder, Rahm saw Naä reach the ground at the light tower's base and run toward Kire, to take his arm. He saw Kire try to shake her off, once—saw her take his shoulder again . . .

Vortcir soared higher, and, beyond the trees and hut roofs, Rahm could see the Myetrans' tents. Moving among them—and occasionally taking off from among them—were not Myetrans, but Winged Ones! Not twenty or thirty, but what seemed hundreds!

"Look there, beside us!" Vortcir called in the wind.

Rahm looked out to his left. By some kind of rope, two Winged Ones pulled something through the air—a kind of glider. It was a larger version of the wood and leather toys Rahm had seen skimming between the flyers in the mountains. Much larger, though—larger than one of the Winged Ones! Piled on the upper side of this one—and there were more of them, many more of them in the air—was a bundle of net. On another was a rack of long-handled knives. On still others, were bound-up balls with spikes jutting from them, whose use Rahm could not even imagine.

"You smell of blood," Vortcir remarked. "But that's better than your skinny friend who stinks of garbage. And—" because, on Vortcir's back, Rahm had started to shake and could now see only shimmering and shifting cloud and light—"you are crying." Though—certainly anyone could hear—they were the grinning sobs of relief.

"What's going to happen to us? Hey, Uk—what's going to happen? I'm bleeding bad! I'm bleeding bad, now—what's going to happen!"

"Shut up, boy—!"

"Shut your mouth—and be quiet!"

"What's going to happen to us? What's going to happen—"

There was a grunt in the darkness. "You want to know what's going to happen? You're going to have a red hot fever by tonight. And in three days that gash in your leg is going to be filled with little white worms. And you're going to have flies crawling all over you. And your mouth's gonna dry up, and you're going to cry for water, only if somebody brings it to you, you won't be able to drink it; and if somebody pours it in your mouth it isn't going to make no difference, and you're gonna hang around like that for seven, eight, nine days, with your tongue cracking and bleeding, turned all black—then you're going to die. That's what's going to happen. An' I just hope I'm dead already when it does—probably will be. Cause what I got's a lot worse than what you do."

"Don't tell him *that*, Uk. You don't have to tell him—"

"Hey, Uk? That's not what's going to happen—is it, Uk? That's not what's gonna happen . . . ? Oh, no—don't tell me that!"

"The boy don't need to know that kind of thing—"

"Then why'd he ask, if he didn't want to know? They pulled their damned blades—when they had us under that net, hacking at us. They didn't cut to kill—you can't fight a war like that! You can't do it like that! That's not the way to do it!"

"They're not going to let that happen to us, are they? You don't think that's what they're going to do? Oh, don't tell me that—"

"You can't pull back when you're fighting like that. If I had my blade, boy, I'd kill you now. Put you out of your misery—and if you don't shut up in here, I may just try it anyway with my bare hands. Only I'm too weak—too bad for you. But keep quiet, I say!"

On the council building's cellar floor, at first making figures like red feathers, blood leaked out to mix with the urine still there from the village prisoners released that morning.

"Oh, don't say that—I'm bleeding, Uk. I'm bleeding so bad—"

"Will you shut up, boy? Are you a man or are you a howling dog? There're men dying in here. And there're going to be more men dying. So will you have some respect and shut up . . . ?"

But after minutes, all form to the red shapes spreading the wet floor was gone.

CHAPTER
SEVEN

From high in the mountains a stream drops in feathery falls, to bubble along beside the grassy fold through the quarry at Çiron.

When Rahm threw a last handful of sand and grit back to pock the water and, elbows high and winging, waded up the bank, his hair was a black sheet bright on his back and his dripping skin was raw—but both were free of blood.

Vortcir perched on a log jutting above the rocks, wings waving like a great moth's.

A leg still in the foamy rush, Rahm looked down to finger up the chain around his neck.

"They were planning to come through the mountains—to Hi-Vator. Hi-Vator was right in their line." Vortcir cocked his head to the side, above his own Handsman's chain. "We heard what they'd done to you and your village. Certainly we couldn't let that happen to us. No sense of weapons, god, or money—you're not far enough along toward civilization for anyone to take you seriously. Still, I did not like these Myetrans—and my aunt said attack. Then, my friend, I heard your name through their accursed speakers—and after that your own call. Well—these are all things to put out of your mind. You are free. Your village is free. A third of the Myetran soldiers run wildly even now, away in the woods. My scouts say most are heading southeast, in the direction of Myetra Himself. More than a third are dead—and the few captured are penned in the basement of your council building. It could be a lot worse."

Along the path to the bank, dappled light spilling bits of even brighter copper down his braids, Abrid ran half a dozen steps, stopped; and, copper spilling hers even faster, Rimgia overtook him. Behind, wings waving in their own rose dapple, the female Winged One who'd once told Rahm about money came after them. "These are the ones you wanted, the two with the red hair—yes, Handsman Rahm? These are the ones, no? Certainly they must be!" Her voice was between a piping and a whine.

"Rahm!" Rimgia declared, Abrid right behind. "The Winged Ones—they drove off the soldiers . . . !" and she began to tell him, excitedly, many things he already knew; and, while Abrid looked excited and kept silent, they started back to the village.

The path crossed the bristle of a burnt field. Halfway over, Rahm stopped. "I'll see thee back in town in a little, Rimgia, at the common," and he turned across the field toward the remains of the shack.

As he came around where half a wall still stood, he stopped.

On her knees, Naä looked up from where she had been pulling earth from under a charred log. "Rahm . . . ?" she smiled up briefly, then dug some more.

Three double handfuls of black, cinder-filled dirt, and she leaned to reach in under with one arm. Sitting back, she lifted free the harp and unwrapped the charred cloth. Two dead leaves were caught in its strings. Fingering them loose, she pulled the base back into her lap, laid her hand against the strings, but did not pluck.

Rather, she reached down to her hip and loosed the knife from her sash. "This is . . . this was Ienbar's." Clearly unsure what to do with it, she held it out to him. "Rahm . . . ?"

He didn't take it; so she put it on the log.

"The children—" Rahm nodded across the field. "Rimgia and Abrid. They're all right. A Winged One found them—"

"Oh!" Suddenly she stood. "They found them—" She smiled at him, looked across the field, at Rahm again—then called: "Rimgia, Abrid . . . !" Pushing her arm through the strap, shrugging the instrument to her back, with Rahm following Naä began to run across the charred grass.

Elbows forward on his knees and gazing at nothing, Lieutenant Kire sat on the blackened block, where he'd been sitting, silent on the common, forty minutes now. The villagers moving about sometimes glanced at him, then—a few and a few more—moved about him without looking at all.

On foot or in air, passing Winged Ones ignored him.

Mantice was chattering away at Rahm as they came across the grass: "Four of them we bandaged up and sent south on their way—though, phew!—they'd only been down there six hours, and already it was halfway between a cesspit and a shambles. One of them—a young fellow—was cut bad in the leg and already down with a fever. But Hara took him into her hut and says she can nurse him back to his feet—although, I allow, he'll limp the rest of his life. But that woman's as wise with medicinal weeds as she is at weaving. If anyone can save him, it'll be she. Three, now, I'm sorry to say it, were too far gone. Two of those were already dead when we went in there. And one died even as we were carrying him up the steps and out into the clear air. Thou wouldst have thought the ones alive and turned loose would have had some gratitude—or at least a smile for the favor. But all of them were sullen fellows. Well, they'd been through it too, I suppose. I had them put the dead ones back over in my water wagon—"

Here the lieutenant looked around, got to his feet heavily, and turned. "Rahm, he says there are more dead about. Myetran dead. In his wagon. May I see them? I . . ." His rough voice snagged on itself. "I've been trying to get an idea whom we lost—among the men I knew, I mean."

"Of course," Rahm said; though, from report, the lieutenant had not done much of anything in the past hour. "Mantice, canst thou take me and friend Kire to see?"

"But only come thou along," said the stocky water cart driver. "My cart is this way."

Five minutes later, off on a side street, with one hand on the wagon's edge, the lieutenant peered within. The puma's head, beside his, save for its sealed eyes, might have been peering too. Standing at Kire's shoulder, Rahm looked in. The lieutenant's next breath was a little louder than the one before it. But the one after was quiet again.

On his back at the cart's far side by three other bodies, the big soldier had a gaping slash along his flank through which, beneath a carapace of flies, you could see both meat and bone. Rahm recognized him more from his size. The full features, unshaven, held a slight grimace in death.

"Friend Kire . . . ?"

"Yes?" The lieutenant looked over, across the lion's muzzle.

"That one there," Rahm said. "Didst thou know him? Was he a bad man . . . ?" though, even as he asked it, the idea of this dead soldier with his annoyed expression, as the evil figure he remembered, seemed ludicrous.

"A bad man?" The lieutenant gave a kind of snort. "Uk, there? Uk was the best—he was a *very* good man. Or at least a good soldier."

"Ah," Rahm said. "I see."

The lieutenant took another, louder breath, dropped his hand, and turned from the cart. "Rahm, I want to thank you, for . . . for my life. Though I guess there's no proper way to give such thanks formally, now, is there . . ."

Rahm grinned. Then he said: "Friend Kire . . ." but nothing else.

So finally Kire said: "I must go and look about among the other men, to see whom I can recognize . . ."

"Certainly."

As the two men turned again toward the common, a young man with his hair tied back hurried up toward them. "Art thou the one they call Lieutenant Kire . . . ?" He was a lean flanked youth, with big ears and big hands. (Rahm grinned at Qualt.) "I was just back at Hara's and Jallet told me—thy prince, he wishes to see thee. Then Hara asked me if I would . . ." While Kire looked uncomfortable, Qualt glanced at Rahm.

"Yes, of course—"

"Thou knowest the house—it's the one they kept thee in, earlier . . . ?"

"Of course," the lieutenant repeated in his unnaturally rough voice, then started back along the street.

When the lieutenant was gone, Qualt resumed his quiet smile: "Hey, Rahm—I heard about him and thee, what thou didst together at the common this morning!"

"And what are we supposed to have done that anyone wouldn't do who had to save himself and a friend?"

"Oh, I heard!" Qualt nodded. "It was a terrifying battle—so says everyone who saw it; and so do a good many more who've only heard of it. Thou gavest the Myetrans a show and a fight, 'ey?"

And Rahm, who had heard nothing at all of what Qualt had done (for even the Winged Ones he'd talked to had not mentioned Qualt by name), put his tree-trunk of an arm about Qualt's lean shoulders and, leaning toward the garbage collector, said: "Well, if thou wouldst talk about it to gossipy old men and women from the back of thy cart when thou makest thy next dawn rounds, let me tell thee a little of what it was *really* like. Here's how it was, for mayhap thou dost not know; but I have even been to Hi-Vator . . . !" and the two youths, Rahm leaning his head down to Qualt's, with Qualt listening and Rahm explicating and gesturing, walked back toward the common.

Minutes later on the same side street, Rimgia and Naä passed Mantice's wagon. Rimgia stood on tip toes, looked in, then turned away with a sour face. "Guess who's in *that* one—" But there was a quick grin, impossible to squelch at the sourness's end. After all, it was not another villager.

"Who—?" Naä asked. She looked too. "Oh . . . *him!* Well, good riddance, I suppose."

"Naä?" Rimgia walked again as again Naä fell in beside her. "Isn't it odd? Yesterday, the idea of what happens when we die seemed just the most fascinating thing in the world to think about. And now, with so many dead about us— our people, theirs—it just seems silly. What, today, dost *thou* think?"

Naä shrugged. "Well, I've always thought

thinking about how to live was more important than thinking about after we die. One likes to assume death will take care of itself. It's just a bit disconcerting to see so many other people putting so much energy into taking care of it for you. Life has always been such a surprise, death, I expect—even if it's nothing—will be one too."

Which, to Rimgia, sounded very wise. The two women walked on through the late afternoon, looking up in the air again and again.

The shack was dark and hot. At one side of the room, blinking about sullenly, a young soldier lay, his leg in a wad of bloody bandage. At the fire, the old weaver glanced up, then went back to stirring her pot over crackling flames. The smell of wintergreen and something vinegary escaped in the steam whipping from the rim.

Some rural remedy, that—however bitter on the tongue, however turgid in the belly—would return the moribund to life?

Or perhaps a country potion, that—if one was lucky, did nothing or, if one was not—hastened the end?

The pallet on the near side was *much* bloodier; and when, from where he lay, the prince began to speak, the young soldier turned away, in disinterest or exhaustion.

"Ah, you've come—it is you, isn't it? I can't see very well. How odd . . . excuse me; this terrible lack of breath, panting—it's all I can do. How odd it is that we have come so near to changing places, you and I. What a very little time ago it was, when, here in this shack in which we were keeping you, you knew that

you'd be dead in hours . . . then in minutes
. . . then, when you were led across the grass,
in moments—and I looked down on it all. Now
I'm the one who knows I have only hours left—
perhaps not even that. And there you stand,
watching, with not much to say. Come here
. . . come closer. We share a mission, you and
I—Ah, when that boy's blade went into my
chest, I could actually feel—beyond the pain,
as I fell, not quite unconscious—I could *feel*
the metal inside, against my heart, feel my
heart beating against the blade, pushing
against the edge that actually touched it, with
each pulse, doubtless cutting itself to ribbons,
even as he wrested it free of my ribs—if I could
only get in a real breath! This panting, like a
woman in labor, just to bring forth my death!
But I wonder if you'll ever know how cursedly
annoying it is to *feel* the inside of your body.
It's quite the strangest thing there is. That
poor, mad Çironian, with his ax—I liked him,
you know? Is it so strange to say? He rather
reminded me of myself—myself a long, long
time ago. I wouldn't be surprised if, years from
now, *he* doesn't begin to remind a few people of
me! Give me your hand there—no, take mine.
Take it . . . did you take it? By Kirke, I can't
even feel it! Really, it's probably him I should
be talking to, not you. Though in all likelihood
he can make the transition—I *trust* he can
make the transition, without my help. I can't
see him staying on here in this town much longer—any more than I can see it for you! They
will be happy to have him, certainly—for a day,
a week, a month even. But he will not be able to
stay here long. Soon he will have to go—of his

own accord, if the town is lucky. Else they will have to drive him out—or kill him: an outlaw in this grotty village with no laws to speak of. For soon they will realize they are harboring that most dangerous creature, a young man who has defied the highest, most rigorous, most rigid law, defied it with mayhem and destruction and most wanton murders—ten, eleven, twelve murders I have heard; thirteen, when I die—and gotten away scot free! No, he must go—even if it takes him a month, a year, five years to be on his way. Really, I would like to be around to observe what happens . . . Come closer, closer. We must be closer, you and I. I can't even see the color of your eyes. Please, you must come closer . . . excuse me for whispering. But I have to conserve my strength—though, for what, I cannot guess. But still—I still feel something separates us, like . . . like what? Like a blood drop run down a . . . Oh, I cannot *tell* you how the notion of eternity bores me—not to mention all the silly stories we're always making up to render the idea palatable! A universe where one has to die is *so* uninteresting—you can understand how we're always flirting with the idea of letting in a bit more evil, then just a bit more—to liven things up. No, come closer. Closer—no . . . this place, in its stinking particularity, doesn't have much of the eternal about it. We're probably in one of those benighted little cultures where every three, five, or seven years, the locals go off on a journey in the wilds, in hopes of becoming a little less local after all. Well, I think that's what *you* probably need, just about now. You were *not* a good officer. But you might still make a good man. I think you would like to be a certain *sort* of man—even, yes, I dare to say it, a good one. But, no, you aren't now. At least not yet. Just ask that boy staring at the thatch, across the room. Or any one of them down in the council-house cellar. Still, to be the man you want to be, you have merely to pursue yourself—passionately, brutally, blindly, looking for no thanks! It means, yes, doing what you feel is right—I have always tried to do what was right. But long ago I learned that being right was a brutal, cruel, and thankless position. Ah—I wish I could see you more clearly! If you pursue yourself in that manner, your friends will criticize you for it, call you a fool—as I have called you. But then, with only a few unhappy moments, I've always considered myself your friend. The things that made you hate me, I only did to shock you, to wake you up, to make you become yourself . . . and you are chuckling bitterly now, saying: *Yes, that's why he condemned me to death!* Well, what we criticize in you, cultivate. That's you. And promise me—promise me, that you will, indeed . . . you will go on to pursue the person you are so close to becoming yet are so far away from. It isn't a very big promise; but I want that promise to fall, like a severing blade, between you and your ever taking the notion for granted that, finally, you have achieved it. For then, my friend, you *will* be in my position—I promise you. So, we have promises to exchange, you and I. Oh, I would love to be able to promise you more than that—more than what is simply inevitable. Come closer, please . . . hold my hand tighter. Don't let anything

hold us apart—not now. Let me do this. Let me
. . . I can't feel you at all. Tighter! A little
tighter? Oh . . . !" The prince made a sudden
attempt to pull air into his ruined ribs that
would not respond. And another. Then, he
whispered: "It's going to *happen*! It's going
to—" For choking moments behind the beard,
his face took on a look of pained surprise, that,
slowly, subsided—till the head dropped to the
side. Bubbles in the red froth at his mouth's
corner burst against beard hair. Breath was
gone.

At the fire, the weaver tapped her long-handled spoon on the cauldron's rim and looked
up. A naked back, with its small, sharp verte-
brae curved toward the room—the young soldier sighed, but did not even glance around.

Across the commons a dog pranced and, its
head back, yipped, till, loping past, Rahm
turned and called jocularly: "Come on, there—
cut it out now, Mouse!"

A child standing near turned to declare: "His
name isn't 'Mouse'—and you *know* it, Rahm!"

Then both laughed—the girl's, a brief, high
sound, like a single note of the dog's yipping,
and Rahm's, a broad-chested, doubled-over,
head-shaking, arm-waving, hand-clapping,
loud-then-high-then-low-again laugh, that
took him three, four, five steps along, going on
and on and *on*—so that, for uncomfortable moments, he looked like a man with a creature
clutching his shoulders whom he was trying to
shake free.

                    *   *   *

Again seated on the edge of the blackened wood, Kire looked at his hysterical savior, as if Kire himself were hundreds of feet above and Rahm, dog, and child were on the ground. His miraculous rescue that dawn had catapulted Kire to some altitude from which, like a man afraid of heights, he could appreciate none of the view for the vertigo. Kire was *still* trying to recall the names of his units' dead—unhappily aware that he could, now, really, remember only one: Nactor, off in the shack. Then, of course, there was his big guard, in the wagon. And what had been the name of his little friend, the one with the freckled shoulders—a soldier Kire knew had died early in the operation, but to whom, for his life, he could now fix neither face nor name. Somehow what had happened to him had so immersed him in life that little of death would stick to him—for which he felt awkward, uncomfortable, and inadequate.

His big body still lost in its laugh, again Rahm glanced at the seated Myetran. Kire looked out with green, distant eyes. Somehow, the dark clothing, with the puma skin around them, had come all askew. I call him 'friend,' Rahm thought. We have now each helped the other; yet I don't know him—at all. And Rahm was glad the laugh's remains kept the thought's discomfort from his face.

The day of the Winged One's coming and their routing of the Myetrans was a day of wonder—wonder that spread from the town dump, where Qualt finally drew up his own wagon with baskets of yellow rinds and chicken feathers and milkslops and egg shells and corn shucks, to go once more, stiff-legged and leaning back against them, over the gravel to dump them from the ravine precipice into the soggy and steaming gully; wonder that spread over the common at the village center, where the grassy expanse was worn away down the middle by the daily set-up of the barter market's stalls just before the council house, where most of the women and many of the men mentioned in these chapters came to walk, judge, and trade; wonder that spread to the outlying grain fields and cane fields and corn fields and kale fields, in one of which Gargula stood, calf deep in greens, beside his plow, rubbing his nose and not quite ready to work, because he'd taken Tenuk's mule from its shed under the thatched-out roof that day, fed it, watered it, and brought it to the field without asking anyone—because there'd been no one to ask; and the whole silent operation had left him with a tongue too heavy to speak.

The wonder and the mystery, as the village children would remember it, was that over all, now on the ground, and more and more frequently in the air, the great shapes, like flitting shadows, moved, awkwardly on the earth and gracefully through the sky, translucent ears cocked left or right to hear, it seemed, everything, their little eyes fixed (it seemed) on little for very long. Thus, as had Naä and Rimgia, one walked about the streets—or the common, or the refuse pit, or the fields—with eyes continually lifting.

Back at the ravine, Qualt smacked the bottom of his last basket, turned it up to peer within its smelly slats, then dragged it behind him, rasping on rock, toward the dozen others, and looked up—as Rimgia came out into the clearing that held his hut as well as his yard full of odd, awkward, and broken things.

She walked thoughtfully, glanced up casually: a dozen Winged Ones circled above the ravine.

Have we mentioned that Qualt, even before the coming of the Myetrans, had for a while, now, been the most respected young man in town? In such a village, the garbage man knows more about what goes on (and goes out) than anyone else. As garbage man, Qualt was expected not just to know this, but to study it, and to record anything about it of interest, which he did two or three evenings a week, on parchment scrolls, with great diligence. It was Qualt who, rather than Rahm, as a child had pestered Old Ienbar to teach him his writing system. In the course of learning it years ago, Qualt had copied out, several times over, almost the whole of the death scrolls on store in Ienbar's shack (he still had those early exercises in trunks piled beneath his grandmothers' marriage blankets in his back storage room), and it was he to whom would soon fall the task of reconstructing them. Hara's jokes with Rahm about a possible seat on the elders' council was a gesture simply to make the big youth feel better. Hara's jokes with Qualt, though they took the same form, were signs of a foregone conclusion of the whole Çiron council, that the lean youth would have the next seat that came vacant—and would be the youngest "elder" ever to sit with them.

Over the next weeks as his various accomplishments during the Myetran siege (from his gathering of information, to his help to Naä, to the water for the prisoners, to the multiple garbage peltings, and finally his own night-journey to Hi-Vator) would come to general awareness, they would make this modest young man into a true town hero—and the already high respect and regard in which he was held would become something quite stellar. What Rahm and Naä had done was the stuff of song. But what Qualt had done was finally the stuff of myth.

At this moment, however, neither Qualt nor Rimgia knew the reputation for heroism that was to accrue. Right now, Qualt was moody, because an hour back he'd had to take his garbage wagon, along with ten other carts (along with Mantice and Brumer and some others), full of corpses, piled so high one or two regularly fell off—soldiers and villagers both—down some two-hundred yards, to dump them into a part of the ravine his predecessor at the dump, years ago, had told him about—the safest place to put corpses when, through man-made or natural catastrophe, the death toll exceeded what the burial meadow might reasonably hold.

The fact and the location were always with him; but this was the first he'd ever had to use it.

Rimgia wandered toward Qualt. Three days ago, she had wanted to make her questions interesting for Naä; but she'd wanted to take the most interesting of their answers to Qualt.

Now, however, as she'd explained to Naä only a bit before, those answers in the aftermath of the violence seemed somehow irrelevant, and so she'd come here feeling oddly empty—yet had come just the same.

Between her fingers, she turned the stem of a black-eyed flower with yellow petals she'd thought to show him; but then, because even that seemed so childish, she threw it to the gravel. And Qualt, because he had seen her father burned down on the common the night before last and had wondered at her mourning, looked at her seriously and said: "Wouldst thou come in? I have some broth heating—I've knocked the marrow from half a dozen pork bones into it . . . ?"

She stepped within the curve of the lean arm he held out, and they walked between the odd junk about his yard. From the Winged Ones flying above, shadows passed and pulled away from them, till, at the door hanging, she turned and looked up, shifting her shoulders under his grip—which he loosened, but did not release. "Qualt, isn't it odd?" she said. "The Winged Ones saved us—saved our whole village. They turned out to be brave and wonderful and generous. Yet we've always been taught to fear them; and now it seems there was no reason to fear. All this time, perhaps we could have been friends with them, learning from them, enjoying their ways and wonders while they benefited from ours. Doesn't that make us seem like a *very* small-minded little village!"

"Perhaps," said thoughtful Qualt. He squeezed her shoulder with his hard, large hand, near permanent in its glove of dirt.

"Dost thou *not* think so?" she asked, looking up—at him and at three (then three more) Winged Ones passing through the luminous space between his long curly hair and the roof's edge.

"Perhaps," he said. "But there still might be reason to fear."

"To fear? The Winged Ones—who saved us? But why?"

Qualt took in a breath, squeezed her shoulder again, and looked slowly at the flying figures around them. "Maybe it's only a little thing—but when it happened, it made me afraid. There was a Winged One who was with me, and whom I thought my friend. And when the Winged Ones came down at our request and were triumphant, and the soldiers had all surrendered, he was with us when we penned some of the Myetrans up in the corral of crossed wires they'd imprisoned some of our people in before. I'd put in both soldiers and officers. And my winged friend now called through the wires, to one of the officers, standing just inside, all in black, still in his hood, with that straight, straight cloak they wear lapping smack to the earth—the only thing that let you know he was a prisoner, really, was that his powergun sling was empty; I'd taken it away from him and smashed it. *Well,* the Winged One wanted to know, *how do you like being a prisoner? Wouldn't it be better to be free? And wouldn't you like to fly, loosed from this cage, free of the fetters of the earth itself?* He kept on teasing him, in his little scrap of a voice. Then, with three flaps to take off, he was up, and inside. *Wouldn't the officer climb on my back, just put an arm around my neck and hold to my shoulder?* I stood outside, grinning as broadly as a child, watching and wishing it was me who'd been offered the ride—that I could change places with him. Myself, I think the officer was afraid at first; and the other soldiers inside the enclosure only looked at the ground. But finally, perhaps because he was also afraid not to, the officer stepped up and put his arms around the Winged One's neck; and, with a few beats of those great wings, making the leaves both inside and outside the fence spin up into the air, they were up among those leaves, then above them, then above the corral itself, moving into the sky, higher, and higher, toward the sun. In less than a minute, they were small as a bird, flying now this way, now that way, against the sky's burning white. Because of the scale, it was hard to tell what was happening; but, I remember, as I watched them, it seemed that the backwards and forwards turnings of that Winged One were awfully quick—dazzlingly fast, faster than I'd seen any of the others fly: a moth about a fire, darting back and about before the sun. Then, I realized the speed was not seemed, but was— for the officer's cape spread and billowed and fluttered and flapped, for the world like a third wing! Had the officer tried to choke the Winged One, perhaps, in his flight? For the Winged One, I realized, was trying to dislodge the man and throw him loose! He flew sideways, he dove head first, then whirled about and rose, now flew upside down, now back again! One thought the officer's cape had gone mad! In no more than thirty seconds, I saw the man tear loose—and fall!

"For the first moments of his plummet, I wondered if my friend might swoop down below him and catch him. But he only flew away. Then, I wondered, if the falling man might spread that cloak and use it, somehow, to fly with—but no. It closed in the air above him, straight over his head. He arrowed down—landing among the trees, some hundred yards off.

"When my companion returned, I was still sure there'd be some explanation—that something had happened on the flight; but no: back on the ground the big fellow was laughing and strutting and boasting to us and all his fellows what a joke it had been; it seemed a joke—to some of them; and to some of them not.

"*But why—?* I asked him at last. *Why did you do it?*

"*He cocked his head at me and said: He was wearing a cape, like the one who seared my wing with his accursed powergun!*

"*But it probably wasn't him,* I told him. *All the officers wear capes. You can't just replace one person for another like that—*

"*But he shrugged his huge shoulders. Well, I wasn't ready to be a ground-bound female, limping along with only one wing and holiness to help me. Why not replace one with the other? Didn't they flog four at random for the mischief of you and me? Oh, I see,* he went on. *I can hear it in your voice. Like all the others—among my people: You're no longer my friend. You don't like me any more. You disapprove. You are afraid. Well, there was no reason to think you'd be otherwise. I'll find some one else to play with.* Then he spread his great wings, with all their scars, and shook them in the sun; and beat them; and flew away.

"But that's when I was afraid."

Rimgia shuddered. "That's terrible!" And after she shuddered, she watched his face, and thought what a sensitive and intelligent young man he was, to have such wonderful feet and hands. "If you wanted to do something like that, it would be better to take one of their dreadful guns and just shoot them through the fence!"

"Mmmm," Qualt said. But it was uncertain if he meant he agreed with her, or merely that he'd heard her. "Later—" Shadows around them became smaller and darker, larger and paler—"I and some of the others went to look at the Myetran who'd fallen among the trees. He'd taken down a lot of branches—and we put his body in a wagon." Always the shadows moved. "As soon as I came back, I ordered the corral to be opened; and I told the soldiers inside to go—it was the corral I was in charge of; I mean, what were we going to do with them? And sullenly they went."

"Mmmm," Rimgia said now, though it was as hard to tell what she meant as it had been when Qualt had said it. Then she said, because it was really why she'd come looking for him in his yard anyway: "Qualt, I like thee—I like thee very much. Dost thou like me?"

"Yes, I . . . Yes . . . yes!" he blurted, stepping away from her to look at her wonderingly, then moving back to hold her tightly in his one arm—even while his other suddenly felt astonishingly empty.

Rimgia looked up at the flying creatures who crossed and parted, and reversed, and lowered, and rose. "Maybe they're not like us," she said. "Maybe they're different."

Qualt said, very carefully: "They are brave and wonderful and generous. They saved our village . . . He did so many things for me—for us. He was my friend—he's *still* my friend. But because they do things that make me so afraid of their difference, that, perhaps, is why we might still be afraid of them a little. But come inside now, Rimgia . . ." He turned with her and pushed back his door hanging. "There's something I must say to thee, must ask thee . . ."

"Whatever is it?" and she stepped within.

Gargula stayed on in the field. Several times, sensing the hour, Tenuk's mule had turned to start back; but Gargula pulled him steady, sometimes with a jerk, staying late for much the reason he had started late.

The first night on the common where Rimgia had lost her father, Gargula had seen an older sister whom he loathed burned till, screaming, she'd fallen dead among so many others screaming—and watched an aunt whom he'd loved far more than his mother trampled by her own friends. Like Rahm, Gargula had spent the night in the fetid and fouled cellar of the council house, that, as a boy, he had helped build. On his release he'd brought dead Tenuk's mule to the field, a man—the only man to go to the fields that day—looking for something. But because the monotonous furrows would not yield it up, he might well have gone on plowing into darkness unto dawn.

What halted him, however, was—well, it was music. But it was also thunder. A house-sized hammer struck among metal mountains might have produced those notes. Then, a voice joined them, but a voice like the sky itself opening up and starting to sing—or *was* it singing?

The mule, then Gargula, stopped.

Before the phrase ended, incomprehensible within its own roar, it collapsed into a laugh— but a laugh as if the whole earth had become woman and was laughing. Finally, there was a voice, with words actually recognizable:

OH, DEAR—! NO, I SOUND *AWFUL*, RAHM!
I'M AFRAID THAT WASN'T A GOOD IDEA AT ALL!
JUST WAIT A MINUTE, WILL YOU?
LET ME SWITCH THIS THING—

Gargula stood, the field a-hum about him.

Then, for whatever reason (not like a man who'd been given what he needed, but like one whom a certain shock had informed that what he needed was not to be found where he was looking), he unhooked the plow and, as the mule twitched a slate colored ear, turned with the animal toward town.

To the west the sky was a wall of indigo, behind mountains whose peaks were crumpled foils, silver and copper. To the east above the tree's back fringe, salmons were layered with purples, separated by streaks the cold color of flame—before which burned and billowed golden clouds. Above in the vault, coming together in yellowish haze, insect tiny, Winged Ones turned, one after the other, to fly toward the rocks.

Gargula walked Tenuk's mule to the path.

As they came out under oak leaves, he heard the visiting singer's voice, harmonizing with her harp-notes. A group had gathered at the well—a number of the village young people who were friends. There was Rimgia, and Abrid, and Qualt. Though he could not see her, certainly Naä sat at their center, on the well wall, singing, playing.

As he looked among the listeners, Gargula saw that Rahm's black hair was now braided down his back—the way you were *supposed* to wear it after you'd come in from a wander. Things, Gargula reflected, were, finally, settling into the ordinary.

And a bit of the weight at the back of his tongue, that had made it too heavy for speech all day, he finally and surprisingly swallowed. (Across the common a line of elders, in their woven robes, walked toward the council building's plank door for that evening's special meeting.) Gargula blinked in the road, at the branches leaning from the underbrush—so that, only when the Myetran officer was three steps away, sling buttoned down over his gun hilt at his leggings' black waist and puma pelt fastened around black shoulders, did Gargula see him.

Without a nod, the lieutenant walked by man and mule, to the south-east, the sun's fire on the puma's lids and bared teeth, on the bronze hair and brown cheek, making him squint—so that Gargula, who turned to watch Kire as he passed, did not even catch the color of his eyes.

—New York/Amherst
June 1962/June 1992

RUINS

Lightning cracked a whip on the dark, scarring it with light.

Clikit ran for the opening, ducked, fell, and landed in dust. Outside, rain began with heavy drops, fast and full. He shook his head, kneeled back, and brushed pale hair from his forehead. Taut, poised, he tried to sense odors and breezes the way, he fancied, an animal might.

There was the smell of wet dirt.

The air was hot and still.

Blinking, he rubbed rough hands over his cheeks, pulling them away when the pain in his upper jaw above that cracked back tooth shot through his head. A faint light came around corners. Clikit kneaded one ragged shoulder. Dimly he could see a broken column and smashed plaster.

Behind him, the summer torrent roared.

He stood, trying to shake off fear, and walked forward. Over the roar came a clap like breaking stone. He crouched, tendons pulling at the backs of his knees. Stone kept crumbling. Beneath the ball of his foot he could feel sand and tiny pebbles—he had lost one sandal hours ago. He stepped again and felt the flooring beneath his bare foot become tile. The strap on his other sandal was almost worn through. He knew he would not have it long—unless he stopped to break the leather at the weak spot and retie it. Clikit reached the wall and peered around cautiously for light.

In a broken frame above, a blue window let in Tyrian radiance. The luminous panes were held with strips of lead that outlined a screaming crow.

Clikit tensed. But over the fear he smiled. So, he had taken refuge in one of the ruined temples of Kirke, eastern god of Myetra. Well, at least he was traveling in the right direction. It was Myetra he had set out for, uncountable days, if not weeks, ago.

In a corner the ceiling had fallen. Water filmed the wall, with lime streaks at the edge. A puddle spread the tile, building up, spilling a hand's breadth, building again, inching through blue light. As he looked down at the expanding reflection of the ruined ceiling, he pondered the light's origin, for—save the lightning—it was black outside.

He walked to the wall's broken end and looked behind for the source—and sucked in his breath.

Centered on white sand a bronze brazier

burned with unflickering flame. Heaped about its ornate feet were rubies, gold chains, damascened blades set with emeralds, silver proof, crowns clotted with sapphires and amethysts. Every muscle in Clikit's body began to shake. Each atom of his feral soul quivered against its neighbor. He would have run forward, scooped up handfuls of the gems, and fled into the wild wet night, but he saw the figure in the far door.

It was a woman.

Through white veils he could see the ruby points of her breasts, then the lift of her hip as she walked out onto the sand, leaving fine footprints.

Her hair was black. Her eyes were blue. "Who are you, stranger?" And her face . . .

"I'm Clikit . . . and I'm a thief, Lady! Yes, I steal for a living. I admit it! But I'm not a very *good* thief. I mean a very bad one. . . ." Something in the expression that hugged her high cheekbones, that balanced over her lightly cleft chin made him want to tell her everything about himself. "But you don't have to be afraid of me, Lady. No, really! Who are—?"

"I am a priestess of Kirke. What do you wish here, Clikit?"

"I was . . ." Dusty and ragged, Clikit drew himself up to his full four-feet-eleven-inches. "I was admiring your jewels there."

She laughed. And the laugh made Clikit marvel at how a mouth could shape itself to such a delicate sound. A smile broke on his own stubbled face, that was all wonder and confusion and unknowing imitation. She said: "Those jewels are nothing to the real treasure of this temple." She gestured toward them with a slim hand, the nails so carefully filed and polished they made Clikit want to hide his own broad, blunt fingers back under his filthy cloak.

Clikit's eyes darted about between the fortune piled before him (and beside him! and behind him!) and the woman who spoke so slightingly of it. Her ebon hair, though the light from the brazier was steady, danced with inner blues.

"Where are you from?" she asked. "Where are you going? And would you like to see the real treasure of the temple?"

"I am only a poor thief, Lady. But I haven't stolen anything for days, I haven't! I live out of the pockets of the rich who stroll the markets of Voydrir, or from what I can find not tied down on the docks of Lehryard, or from what is left out in the gardens of the affluent suburbs in Jawahlo. But recently, though, I've heard of the wealth of Myetra. I only thought I would journey to see for myself. . . ."

"You are very near Myetra, little thief." Absently she raised one hand, thumb and forefinger just touching, as if she held something as fine as the translucent stuffs that clothed her.

And dirty Clikit thought: It is my life she holds, my happiness, my future—all I ever wanted or all I could ever want.

"You must be tired," she went on, dropping her hand. "You have come a long way. I will give you food, rest; moreover, I shall display for you our real treasure. Would you like that?"

Clikit's back teeth almost always pained him, and he had noticed just that morning that another of his front ones (next to the space left from the one that had fallen out by itself a month ago) was loose enough to move with his tongue. He set his jaw hard, swallowed, and opened his mouth again. "That's . . . kind of you," he said, laying two fingers against his knotted jaw muscle, eyes tearing with the pain. "I hope I have the talents to appreciate it."

"Then follow. . . ." She turned away with a smile he desperately wanted to see again—to see whether it was a taunting one at him, or a glorious one for him. What he remembered of it, as he trotted after her, had lain in the maddeningly ambiguous between.

Then he glanced down at her footprints. Fear shivered in him. Alabaster toe and pink heel had peeked at him from under her shift. But the prints on the white sand were not of a fleshed foot. He stared at the drawn lines—was it some great bird's claw? No, it was bone! A skeleton's print!

Stooping over the clawlike impression, Clikit thought quickly and futilely. If he went to search along the walls for pebbles and stones and fallen chunks of plaster, she would surely see. At once he swept up one, another, and a third handful of sand into his cloak; then he stood, gathering the edges together, twisting the cloak into a club—which he thrust behind him. At another arch the woman turned, motioning him to follow: he was shaking so much he didn't see if she smiled or not. Clikit hurried forward, hands at his back, clutching the sandy weight.

As he crossed the high threshold, he wondered what good such a bludgeon would do if she were really a ghost or a witch.

Another brazier lit the hall they entered with blue flame. He went on quickly, deciding that at least he must try. But as he reached her, without stopping she looked over her shoulder. "The real treasure of this temple is not its jewels. They are as worthless as the sands that strew the tile. Before the true prize hidden in these halls, you will hardly think of them . . ." Her expression had no smile in it at all. Rather, it was intense entreaty. The blue light made her eyes luminous. "Tell me, Clikit—tell me, little thief—what would you like more than all the jewels in the world?" At a turn in the passage, the light took on a reddish cast. "What would you like more than money, good food, fine clothes, a castle with slaves. . . ."

Clikit managed a gappy grin. "There's very little I prefer over good food, Lady!"—one of his most frequent prevarications. There were few foods he could chew without commencing minutes of agony, and it had been that way so long that the whole notion of eating was, for him, now irritating, inevitable, and awful.

A hint of that smile: "Are you really so hungry, Clikit . . . ?"

True. With the coming of his fear, his appetite, always unwelcome, had gone. "I'm hungry enough to eat a bear," he lied, clutching the sand-filled cloak. She looked away . . .

He was about to swing—but she turned through another arch, looking back.

Clikit stumbled after. His knees felt as though the joints had come strangely loose. In this odd yellow light her face looked older. The lines of character were more like lines of age.

"The treasure—the real treasure—of this

temple is something eternal, deadly and death-
less, something that many have sought, that
few have ever found."

"Eh . . . what is it?"

"Love," she said, and the smile, a moment
before he could decide its motivation, crumbled on her face into laughter. Again she
turned from him. Again he remembered he
ought to bring his bundle of sand up over his
own balding head and down on the back of
hers—but she was descending narrow steps.
"Follow me down."

And she was, again, just too far ahead. . . .

Tripods on the landings flared green, then
red, then white—all with that unmoving glow.
The descent, long and turning and long again,
was hypnotic.

She moved out into an amber-lit hall. "This
way. . . ."

"What do you mean—love?" Clikit thought
to call after her.

When she looked back, Clikit wondered:
Was it this light, or did her skin simply keep its
yellowish hue from the light they had passed
through above?

"I mean something that few signify by the
word, though it hides behind all that men seek
when they pursue it. I mean a state that is eternal, unchangeable, imperturbable even by
death . . ." Her last word did not really end. Its
suspiration, rather, became one with the
sound of rain hissing through a broken roof in
some upper corridor.

Now! thought Clikit. Now! Or I shall never
find my way out! But she turned through another arch, and again his resolve fled. She was

near him. She was away from him. She was facing him. She was facing him. She faced away. Clikit stumbled through a narrow tunnel low of ceiling and almost lightless. Then there was green, somewhere . . .

A flood of green light. . . .

Again she turned. "What would you do with such a treasure? Think of it, all around you, within you, without you, like a touch that at first seemed so painful you thought it would sear the flesh from your bones but that soon, you realized, after years and years of it, was the first you had ever known of an existence without pain. . . ."

The green light made her look . . . older, much older. The smile had become a caricature. Where, before, her lips had parted faintly, now they shriveled from her teeth.

"Imagine," and her voice made him think of sand ground in old cloth, "a union with a woman so all-knowing she can make your mind sink towards perfect fulfillment, perfect peace. Imagine drifting together down the halls of night, toward the shadowy heart of time, where pure fire will cradle you in its dark arms, where life is a memory of evil at once not even a memory . . ." She turned away, her hair over her gaunt shoulders like black threads over stone. "She will lead you down halls of sorrow, where there is no human hunger, no human hurt, only the endless desolation of a single cry, without source or cessation. She will be your beginning and your end; and you will share an intimacy more perfect than the mind or body can endure . . ."

Clikit remembered the burden clutched behind him. Was it lighter? He felt lighter. His brain floated in his skull, now and again bumping against the portals of perception at eye or ear. And they were turning. She was turning.

". . . leading toward perfect comprehension in the heart of chaos, a woman so old she need never consider pain, or concision, or life. . . ."

The word pierced him like a mouse fang.

Clikit pulled his cloak from behind him and swung it up over his shoulder with cramped forearms. But at that instant she turned to face him. Face? . . . No face! In blue light black sockets gaped from bald bone. Tattered veils dropped from empty ribs. She reached for him, gently taking an edge of his rags between small bone and bone. Empty?

His waving cloak was empty! The sand had all trickled through some hole in the cloth.

Struggling to the surface of his senses, Clikit whirled, pulled away, and fled along the hall. Laughter skittered after him, glancing from the damp rock about him.

"Come back, my little thief. You will never escape. I have almost wrapped my fingers around your heart. You have come too far . . . too far into the center—" Turning a corner, Clikit staggered into a tripod that overturned, clattering. The steady light began to flicker. "You will come back to me. . . ." He threw himself against the wall, and because for some reason his legs would not move the way he wanted, he pulled himself along the rocks with his hands. And there was rain or laughter.

And the flickering dimmed.

* * *

A tall old woman found him huddled beside her shack door next day at dawn.

Wet and shivering, he sat, clutching his bare toes with thick, grubby fingers, now and again muttering about his sandal strap—it had broken somewhere along a stone corridor. From under a dirty, thinning tangle like cornsilk, his grey gaze moved slowly to the tall woman.

First she told him to go away, sharply, several times. Then she bit her lower lip and just looked down at him awhile. Finally, she went back into the shack—and came out, minutes later, with a red crock bowl of broth. After he drank it, his talk grew more coherent. Once, when he stopped suddenly, after a whole dozen sentences that had actually made a sort of sense to her, she ventured:

"The ruins of Kirke's temple are an evil place. There are stories of lascivious priestesses walled up within the basement catacombs as punishment for their lusts. But that was hundreds of years ago. Nothing's there now but mice and spiders."

Clikit gazed down into the bowl between his thumbs.

"The old temple has been in ruin for over a century," the woman went on. "This far out of the city, there's no one to keep it up. Really, we tell the children to stay away from there. But every year or so some youngster falls through some unseen hole or weak spot into some crypt, to break an arm or leg." Then she asked: "If you really wandered so far in, how did you find your way out?"

"The sand . . ." Clikit turned the crock,

searching among the bits of barley and kale still on its bottom. "As I was stumbling through those corridors, I saw the trail of sand that had dribbled through my cloak. I made my way along the sandy line—sometimes I fell, sometimes I thought I had lost it—until I staggered into the room where I had first seen the . . ." His pale eyes lifted. ". . . the jewels!"

For the first time the old woman actually laughed. "Well, it's too bad you didn't stop and pick up some of that 'worthless treasure' on your way. But I suppose you were too happy just to have reached open air."

"But I did!" The little man tugged his ragged cloak around into his lap, pulling and prodding at the knots in it. "I did gather some . . ." One knot came loose. "See . . . !" He pulled loose another.

"See what?" The tall woman bent closer as Clikit poked in the folds.

In the creases was much fine sand. "But I—" Clikit pulled the cloth apart over his lap. More sand broke out and crumbled away as he ran his fingers over it. "I stopped long enough to put a handful of the smaller stones in. Of course, I could take nothing large. Nothing large at all. But there were diamonds, sapphires, and four or five gold lockets set with pearls. One of them had a great black one, right in . . ." He looked up again. ". . . the middle . . ."

"No, it's not a good place, those ruins." Frowning, the woman bent closer. "Not a good place at all. I'd never go there, not by myself on a stormy summer night."

"But I did have them," Clikit repeated. "How

did they—? Where did they—?"

"Perhaps—" The woman started to stand but stopped, because of a twinge along her back; she grimaced—"your jewels trickled through the same hole by which you lost your sand."

The man suddenly grasped her wrist with short, thick fingers. "Please, take me into your house, Lady! You've given me food. If you could just give me a place to sleep for awhile as well? I'm wet. And dirty. Let me stay with you long enough to dry. Let me sleep a bit, by your stove. Maybe some more soup? Perhaps you— or one of your neighbors—has an old cloak. One without so many holes? Please, Lady, let me come inside—"

"No." The woman pulled her hand away smartly, stood slowly. "No. I've given you what I can. It's time for you to be off."

Inside the tall old woman's shack, on a clean cloth over a hardwood table, lay sharp, small knives for cutting away inflamed gums, picks for cracking away the deposits that built up on teeth around the roots, and tiny files—some flat, some circular—for cleaning out the rotten spots that sometimes pitted the enamel, for the woman's position in that hamlet was akin to a dentist's, an art at which, given the primitive times, she was very skilled. But her knives and picks and files were valuable, and she had already decided this strange little man was probably a wandering thief fallen on hard times—if not an outright bandit.

A kind woman, she was, yes; but not a fool. "You go on, now," she said. "I don't want you to come in. Just go."

"If you let me stay with you a bit, I could go

back. To the temple. I'd get the jewels. And I'd give you some. Lots of them. I would!"

"I've given you something to eat." She folded her arms. "Now go on, I said. Did you hear me?"

Clikit pushed himself to his feet and started away—not like someone who'd been refused a request, the woman noted, but like someone who'd never made one.

She watched the barefooted little man hobble unsteadily over a stretch of path made mud by rain. As a girl, the old woman had been teased unmercifully by the other children for her height, and she wondered now if anyone had ever teased him for his shortness. A wretch like that, a bandit? she thought. Him? "You'll be in Myetra in half a day if you stay on the main road," she called. "And keep away from those ruins. They're not a good place at all. . . ." She started to call something else. But then, if only from his smile and the smell, when she'd bent over his cloak, those teeth, she knew, were beyond even *her* art.

She watched him a minute longer. He did not turn back. In the trees behind her shack a crow cawed three times, then flapped up and off through the branches. She picked up the red bowl, overturned on the wet grass, and stepped across the sand, drying in the sun, to go back inside and wait for whichever of the townsfolk would be the first of the day's clients.

—New York, 1962

RETURN TO ÇIRON

*W*hen he was an old man and the Calvi-con historian sought him out in his hut outside the fishing village with the sea below gnawing at the stones, one evening after they'd gone over yet again the organization and exploits of the Myetran army, he began to speak of something unmentioned in their previous conversations.

When I left him there, my prince and leader, dead in the old peasant woman's shack, I had the strangest feeling—as though I . . . were no I at all. Ah, I wish I could find some trace of the 'I' I was then—you understand, there are moments when it seems it would solve so many problems today. But that old self has been all but squeezed out of existence, between my total absence of self at the time and my own voice and consciousness exploring the ashy detritus of that time now—I don't know: *can* you put yourself in my place . . . ? Not my place today: the place I occupied then. I had seen my executioner revealed as my savior and, only a breath of time on, had watched my mentor—who had been, of course, my *real* executioner—die. Well, as I left him in the stifling, peasant's hovel, to step into the light and air, I thought, again, that I must return to our camp and make one more try to get an idea of the damages, if only in terms of names.

But the last time I'd been taken from the camp to the execution site, I'd been bound, it had been dark; nor had my mind really been on the route we followed. Thus the village was, for me, a wholly unknown landscape. At one point I turned from an alley, to step through some trees I thought must put me out at the Myetran camp after only thirty or forty paces—and after eighty or a hundred, about convinced I was lost, came out at the edge of a field, covered with charred patches, like ashy lakes, several of them joined to one another. On the far side, I saw a scattering of what had to be corpses—from the carrion birds swirling above them: at this distance, they were the size of flies. A wagon stood among them. To one side, between some trees, were the burnt ruins of a shack.

Near me, on the grass, where I'd emerged, the first thing I saw was a vine web—like the one that had saved us on the town common. This one was staked out at one edge along the ground. Then, it slanted upward toward a

branch of gnarly oak. Bales of that vine webbing lay about, higher than my waist. Against
another tree, one of their gliders leaned. Two
others sat on the ground.

On the branch where the net went, a Winged
One perched. Another squatted on the ground,
wings sloping out across the green and ashy
stubble. As I stood, a third flew down, into the
web, caught the vines, pulled in those great
sails, and turned back to stare at me—then
laughed, with the most shrill and astonishing
Screeee!

I had no idea if they'd attack or let me pass.
But the one on the ground suddenly looked up
and cried: "Play a game with us, groundling!
Play a game . . . !"

The one on the branch mewed distractedly,
glancing at the sky: "We are here to play with
the hero . . . !"

"But the hero is away, playing a hero's
games, with the prisoners and the victorious
villagers!" declared the one who'd arrived at
the net. "Perhaps you will let us play with
you . . . ?"

"What do you mean?" I asked. "What . . . sort
of game?"

"A game of desire," said the one clinging.

Knowingly, the one perched looked down.
"A *sexual* game . . ."

The one squatting said: "Climb on my back!
Let me fly with you, just a little ways—just a
short flight . . . just enough . . . !"

I'd seen my friend take off and land, on the
back of Handsman Vortcir. Who, so seeing,
could not covet such flight!

Also, I suppose, I was afraid not to. For they were so strong—they'd just vanquished the whole of a Myetran brigade!

These particular three, you understand—well, I was not even sure if they were females; though, now, I assume so. But it was hard to tell. Certainly they were younger members of their tribe. And clearly they brought an enthusiasm, if not an avidity, to their play.

I bent to take the back of the one who squatted.

The wings pulled in, rose, opened, and fell—and I was born up, grabbing at the great shoulders.

And what was the game?

Now—now, in the air, I was to transfer to the back of one of the others! But how in the world—?

Just do it!

First, one came close. I threw my arms around the neck of one flying so near their four wings beat each others'. And I was pulled away, to hang, till, at a certain maneuver, we flew upside down—and I lay with my carrier, belly to belly, looking at that strange smile, just under mine!

Then, again, when I was not really holding, I was rolled loose and actually fell, my heart blocking my throat with its beats, as if my head were back on the block, to land on the back of the third—and I scrambled over, to grasp and hold the shoulders, while we sagged down with my added weight and recovered, while the others, flying just above, mewed caressive reassurances: now I was urged to leap, myself, from the one I rode to one who flew just under us; and—rather than be thrown again—in a perfect panic I leaped; and was caught between those billowing leathers. They passed me among them, while, between the wings of one and the wings of another, the village lay hundreds of feet below. Next time I looked, the stubbled field passing back beneath was so near—not a full two feet under us, every daisy and grass blade and burnt twig speeding clearly—I was sure we'd wreck ourselves on the smallest rise. We lifted again. Somehow, I was tossed, again, for a last time—and caught, in the net, on my back.

They swarmed over me!

One pulled loose my waist cinch, another the fastenings on my jerkin. They mewed into my ears such things as: "We play the game of desire, along the chain of desire, serving the Winged One's Queen! We serve the beloved of the Queen, who is the Handsman. We serve the beloved of the Handsman, who is the brave groundling. We serve the beloved of the brave groundling, who is the groundling's black clad friend . . . We tangle the chain in our play!" One piece and another, my clothes came away, till all that was under my naked back was the harsh uncured skin—and, folded over it, the wondrously soft fur—of the puma.

The three of them at me, there, shook me and pleasured me, bit at me—yes, in several places, my shoulder, my inner thigh, they sipped blood—while I rebounded in the web.

Do you understand? Moments before, I had been by a dying man, with whom I'd constantly felt I was not present to his words—a man who had urged me to exchange promises with him,

as if we'd been a pair of lovers, yet, to whose
urgings, my own perceptions had been so
blighted I could not tell if he knew or not I was
unable to respond, for he might as well have
been addressing the lion skull, already dead,
by mine.

But now, with these three lovers upon me,
my bodily perceptions were cajoled, caressed,
excited to a pitch, an altitude, where language
could not follow, so that promises themselves
were impossible. As I floated and flowed and
soared above words, listening to their mewings
and scrittings, I let a sound that was wholly
animal, as inhuman as if the beast's skull beside me had, for a moment, returned to life.

I slid, finally, down the web. On the burned
earth, when, at last, I could stand, I looked
about for my cloths, pulled on my leggings, my
boots, my gloves.

The three Winged Ones all perched on the
branch, as indifferent to my fumblings below
with belt hooks, boot laces, and button fastenings as lords of the air might be.

I threw the puma skin over my back and, fastening it, stumbled off into the trees—unable
to look back, bereft of all my initial desire: to
survey the damages among my troops.

I only remembered it when I was again walking between the shacks in some narrow alley.
Reaching the end, I saw I was back at the common—with no progress at all in my project.

But perhaps you can understand why this is
not an event I often tell. Really, I can't think
how it concerns your own researches. It might,
if you have any sense of delicacy, be better left

unmentioned. As I said, put yourself in my place . . .

In evening light, the Calvicon historian listened to the little stones which the waves raked away, then, returning, flung up the shingle. He sipped from his drink and nodded (for the historian was tired, and, as they'd sat in the small yard, his host had refilled both their glasses several times), not certain just what he'd been asked.

—Amherst
September 1991

THE BEST OF FANTASY FROM TOR

☐ 51175-1 *ELVENBANE* $5.99
       Andre Norton & Mercedes Lackey $6.99 Canada

☐ 53503-0 *SUMMER KING, WINTER FOOL* $4.99
       Lisa Goldstein $5.99 Canada

☐ 53898-6 *JACK OF KINROWAN* $5.99
       Charles de Lint $6.99 Canada

☐ 50249-3 *SISTER LIGHT, SISTER DARK* $3.95
       Jane Yolen $4.95 Canada

☐ 51099-2 *THE GIRL WHO HEARD DRAGONS* $5.99
       Anne McCaffrey $6.99 Canada

☐ 51965-5 *SACRED GROUND* $5.99
       Mercedes Lackey $6.99 Canada

THE BEST OF FANTASY FROM TOR